Mythic Survivor

Afterlife Quest: Mae Trilogy - Book One

M. Declan Morris

ISBN: 979-8-9996640-0-6

CONTENTS

Dedicated to my mother.

Acknowledgements

A special thank you to everyone who has read my books and has supported my creativity and heart for mental wellness. Thank you, early readers: Matthew, Christopher, Jamie, Jaeden, and Cimarron.

This book is about a domestic abuse survivor. I understand that this is a difficult subject and potential trigger, so I asked a friend of mine who is a licensed marriage and family therapist to write a forward.

A colossal thank you to Jennifer Camareno.

FOREWORD

I first met Michael in 2023 as we joined forces with a few other 30-somethings to fulfill the mission of our own adventure: to track down young adults in their various scattered and lonely positions in relation to church, and usher them into something that better resembled a family, with all the conflict, potential for pain, and yet hope of redeemed love that that analogy conjures.

As I got to know Michael, I was struck by his ability to both learn and teach. He is a keen observer, translating his findings into words that anyone can understand. As we shared messages of hope with older teens and 20-somethings, Michael's relatability and insight gave our young adults something they could hold onto.

Michael's compassion combined with his powers of observation and learning have provided the foundation for this series. Here he deals with heavy topics such as PTSD and domestic violence from a curious and creative standpoint. It's not often that an author tackles both learned helplessness and how to defeat mythological monsters in one text, though as we flip through the pages of this book we gain much as to how to conquer the monsters within us that have taken on mythological proportions in our own lives.

Michael bravely ventures into frightening experiences like nightmares and flashbacks. He reveals how speaking out your own story in the context of an empathic relationship provides the context for real healing of the soul. In this story we bare witness as Mae moves from isolation to friendship, and we are invited out of our own emotional hiding places into the light of human connection. We watch as Mae takes a more active stance in her daunting world, confronting the creatures that would cause her own and others' destruction. And once again we are invited to move with Mae from a position of defeated victimhood to a belief that our own voice and choices matter. As we resonate with Mae's suppressed anger towards her abuser, we discover that our own stifled rage must be allowed to find its voice and worked through to a posture of deeper vulnerability, agency, and eventually boundaried compassion. Though the healing journey is no walk in the park, each of us is capable of seeking and finding the internal and external resources that can revitalize us.

Michael's sincere hope in the writing of this series is that it spurs readers on to their own mental wellness. As you follow Mae through her adventures, may you be empowered to live your own adventures with courage and hope. Life awaits.

Jennifer Camareno,
Licensed Marriage and Family Therapist, ID MFT-8238, CA MFT-90338

Acheron Peaks

Dardis

Pelasgos Valley

Melosia

Mistion Sea

Lake Narcis

Taygetian Wilds

Olympus

Thermos

River Styx

Erimos

Hades

Elysian Wilds

Naxion Sea

Neos Ellas

Cythara

Chapter 1

Don't Panic

"The question is asked, what proof you could give if anyone should ask us now, at the present moment, whether we are asleep and our thoughts are a dream, or whether we are awake and talking with each other in a waking condition?"

The words from one of Plato's works passed through my groggy mind like a passing train. I read a lot of Ancient Greek wisdom literature. Probably in a misguided attempt to justify my life's choices. I mentally waved at the passing thought as it faded away, back into the recesses of my elderly brain. I opened my eyes and my other senses kicked in. This made me realize that I was lying down.

The ceiling was unfamiliar to me. Which a strange observation, but still frightening. I'd just woken up with fear and confusion trying to win top position in my mind and it was a game that I didn't want played. As my eyes adjusted to the lighting above me, I saw a figure in my peripheral vision. The figure was sitting beside the bed I was lying in. I felt a railing of some sort protecting me from falling out of the bed. A hospital bed? That would explain the noises.

The soft hum of machinery echoed in the room, the rhythmic beeping of the heart monitor filled the silence. I turned my head just enough to see the sky outside the window. It was painted with streaks of deep orange and violet, signaling the end of another day. Maybe my last day. I tried to push that idea away, but the nagging reality of the situation was punctuated by the high-pitched beep which seemed to be slowing down.

Memories flooded back unbidden. It was like watching a slideshow, which wasn't great anyway, but especially not in this situation. The images passed so quickly as decades of love, pain, and heartache cascaded past my mind's eye. I'd heard about a person's life flashing before their eyes, but I didn't think that literally was what happened.

"Uh oh," I said weakly. "That can't be good." The words barely made a sound and I knew that I had few words left. I better make them count. I felt a person grab my hand and give it a gentle squeeze. I knew I was in trouble when even the light pressure caused me pain.

"I'm here, mom," a voice said. I turned my head toward the voice, even though the movement also hurt. It was the voice of my son and I wanted to see him.

"I love you, David," I said as my tear ducts mustered for their final performance. My weak, dehydrated body wasn't giving them much to work with and they'd been overstressed for the majority of my life in the first place. I was happy for them to finally be able to retire, though not thrilled at the reason why I wouldn't have need of their services soon. I was about to die. I understood this fact from the core of my being. I had a strange peace about dying. I couldn't explain it.

I lay in the bed, my frail body tucked beneath a thin, sterile sheet. My world was beginning to dim. My half-lidded eyes would fail before the unwavering, cold hospital lights. I knew the lighting issue was on my end. I felt the weight of my age and the finality of my earthly journey. My skin felt loosely stretched across delicate bones. My breath was shallow, each exhale a whisper of life, which grew softer with each passing moment.

David sat in a stiff, uncomfortable looking chair beside me. His hands, large and rough like his father's, held my smaller, trembling hand. The years had weathered him, just as they had me. His hair had long since turned gray, and the wrinkles on his face emphasized the worry and love he felt for his mother. Despite his stoic demeanor, his eyes betrayed the sadness he tried to suppress. He wasn't ready to let me go, even though he knew this day had been coming for months.

"I'm here, Mom," he whispered again, his voice thick with emotion. "I'm right here. I love you."

My lips moved slightly to respond, but no sound came out. My mind, once sharp and lively, now drifted in and out of clarity. I couldn't speak. The room around me began to feel distant, as though I was slipping between two worlds. I could still sense David's presence beside me, but my thoughts wandered far from the hospital bed. Memories of a long and difficult life tugged at my consciousness. Some of these memories I had tried to forget, but which now seemed to surface as if to demand resolution.

I saw him again. My husband. The man I had once loved so fiercely, before the war stole him from me. Before the violence, before the anger, before the nights spent hiding bruises from friends, and before the days filled with silence that spoke louder than any words. I had stayed, loyal and patient, hoping that one day he would return to the man I had married. But he never did. Should I have left? Where would I have gone? The war had broken him in ways neither of us saw coming. In the end, it had broken me too.

I had tried to be a good mother, but I didn't know the best way to raise a son with an abusive father. David had experienced too much emotionally as a child, and it had shaped him in ways I regretted. I could see the burden in his eyes even now, the unspoken questions he still carried about his family's history and about his father. The guilt weighed on me, even in these final moments.

"Mom, it's okay," he said, as if sensing my turmoil. As if he knew that my life had just replayed before me. I had been gifted with a brief moment of clarity, where David came back into full focus. "You don't have to say anything. You did your best and I love you."

A final, soft tear slipped from the corner of my eye. I had so much to say to him. So much I wished I had said years ago. But the words felt trapped inside me, tangled in the pain I had spent a lifetime trying to hide. I felt powerless. It wasn't a new feeling for me. I had felt powerless for most of my life. I guess it was a fitting end.

The hospital room was fading, the sound of the heart monitor growing distant. The smell of antiseptic and the soft murmur of nurses in the hallway became less distinct. My vision blurred, but in the haze, I saw something else. A flicker of golden light, faint at first, then growing brighter. This was different from the hospital lights.

I blinked, and suddenly the room felt warmer, softer, as if the air had shifted. The pain in my chest, which had been constant for days, began to ease. My hand, still clasped in David's, seemed to grow lighter. I tried to focus on him, to hold on to this moment, but the light in the corner of my vision beckoned, drawing me toward it.

The edges of reality blurred. Time stretched and I felt as though I was floating. The pain, the fear, and the memories all seemed to dissolve into the light.

"Mom?" David's voice was a distant echo now, as though he were speaking from across a vast chasm. I wanted to respond, to reassure him, but I was no longer there. I was slipping away, the golden light pulling me forward. The light kept getting brighter, eventually losing its golden hue and shifting to bright white. It encompassed everything.

For a moment, there was nothing except the light. Only silence. Then a breath. A soft, final exhale.

I felt weightless. It was like I was floating in space. However, instead of an endless dark void, everything was the blinding white light. I had no reference for the passage of time and no idea how long I had been floating. I felt pressure under me and was in a seated position as the light began to fade.

As my eyes adjusted to my surroundings, I saw that I was in a white room. It was different from the hospital though. The light was emanating from behind a large wood desk. The figure of a man became more clear as the light continued to fade. It wasn't David.

"Mae June Cohen," said the man who was dressed in all white.

I had difficulty parsing what was happening, since it was such a shift from my previous reality. I understood the man had just said my name, but I didn't understand what had just transpired.

"You have died," continued the man in white.

"That does seem like it would be the most logical explanation," I said. After a moment of brief silence I had to ask the question that was burning in my mind. "Is this heaven?"

"No," the man said as a grin spread across his face. My next thought frightened me and he must've seen the change. He quickly added, "It isn't Hell either."

I took a deep breath in relief. "Okay, well I was recently an elderly woman dying in a hospital bed and now I'm pain free sitting before you. It's not that I'm ungrateful, but an explanation would be greatly appreciated."

"Certainly, Mrs. Cohen. You are currently in what some might call purgatory. Although it isn't to rid you from impurities per se. Think of it more as a place to process the things you need to from your time on Earth in order to have a positive experience with what comes next," he explained.

"Just Mae is fine, dear. What I'm hearing is that it's to my benefit to go along with this process and there is nothing to worry about eternity-wise?" I asked. For whatever reason, I felt comfortable with the man in white. He spoke in such a way that it was easy to trust him. It reminded me of chatting with an old friend.

"It is definitely beneficial. Imagine going into eternity with a rock in your shoe that you are unable to remove. It would eventually destroy you given what would equate to thousands of years of gradually increasing pain and irritation. This place, and even more so the place where you are about to be, is an opportunity to take care of the issue. I want to help you remove the rock," he said, with reassuring confidence.

"I guess the next questions I would have are: Where am I going next? And what is the rock I need to extract?" I asked. I was genuinely curious about his choice of words. It all seemed too good to be true, honestly.

He smiled and just looked at me for a moment as if savoring a surprise he was about to share. "I'm excited to tell you about the place, but it isn't in your best interest for me to explain the rock. Some things are better discovered than told."

"Well, I'm an old woman! Don't keep me waiting," I said playfully.

He gave a soft laugh and said, "I don't think age or time is going to be an issue. Why don't you have a quick look at your hands?"

I raised my hands in front of my face and looked them over, front and back. These weren't the hands that had been giving me trouble for the last twenty plus years. These were the strong hands of a twenty-year-old or maybe a thirty-year-old. I had been old for that many years and couldn't remember them looking this good. "I'm young again?"

"You are in what you would call your 'prime'. Don't panic though. You get to keep all of the mental maturity and wisdom from all your years on Earth," said the man in white with a smile.

"Am I ready to go to whatever this exciting place is?" I asked.

"Yes," he said. The smile was back on his face. "I have prepared something very special for you and am giving you a gift that few receive in these situations. You will be going on an adventure in a land inspired by ancient Greek mythology. I don't want to spoil any of the surprises, so I won't tell you more."

I was so excited by the reveal that I almost forgot to ask what the gift that few receive was. The little kid in me won out and I asked. "Okay, what's the gift?" I felt like a young child at Christmas when the words came out of my mouth.

"Invincibility," he said, as if that wasn't impossible for a 'fragile-my-whole-existence' human brain to imagine.

"You mean like a god?" I asked.

"As far as your understanding of the ancient Greek pantheon goes, that would be a way of understanding the power. Let's just call those with godlike powers a name that takes the connection to deity out of the picture. We'll call them Mythics. You've read enough about the ancient Greek pantheon to know that they were very human in their decision-making and very much flawed beings. Man-made ideas to represent the reality around them," he said, matter-of-factly.

"Am I going to be one of these Mythics then?" I asked. I had many more questions, but didn't want to lose my gift due to annoying the obviously powerful being before me. I mean, anyone who can hand out invincibility has got to be pretty powerful.

"Not exactly. How about I give a little nudge and you take it from there? No one will know who you are, even the Mythics. You will have complete freedom to figure out how your story will go. I ask you to trust me with one of my decisions though. As a way of helping you, although you may not always like it, while you are in this new world you'll have visions when you sleep of your life on Earth. These will be there to help you figure out your purpose for the adventure. I'll visit from time to time to help if you need another little nudge and you'll have some other helpers here and there as well," said the man in white as he stood and began to walk around the desk. I stood as he approached.

"What's the first little nudge?" I asked. As I stood and finally got a good look at the white room I was in, I noticed that all four walls surrounding us were blank. No windows and no doors. I looked back at the man next to me for answers.

"I'll lead you to the door and I'll help you with the first step," he said.

"What door?" I asked, motioning to the bare walls.

"That door," he said, pointing to the now present door in the middle of the wall behind me. He walked over to it, turned the knob, and a bright light came through as it went from a crack to fully open.

I was so excited about the possibility of stepping into what had always been my favorite subject that I didn't even care about the sudden magic carpentry trick. I loved ancient Greek mythology and wisdom. My favorite quotes were from ancient Greek poets and philosophers. I got to the final step right before I'd cross over the door's threshold and paused. "What about the little nudge?"

The man in white stood behind me as the light streamed in, outlining my excitedly confused body. "Are you ready?" He asked. I nodded without a second thought. I felt a gentle push that was just enough to get me to take a step through the mystery door. My foot found no flooring on the other side of the threshold and my body began to fall forward. Once my whole body was through the door, I realized that I was falling. It was more than just a little tumble, I was hurtling through the air. Was this all a sick joke? Was this how they sent people to the non-Heaven option?

I saw land below me, but the wind was rushing by my face with too much force to allow for a good inspection of my surroundings. The slight spin didn't help either. The last thought that ran through my mind as I fell, was that whatever the outcome of this freefall, I was about to make an impact on this place.

Chapter 2

PELASGOS VALLEY

I tumbled through the air, my arms flailing wildly as I plummeted. I guess it wasn't to my death though, right? A dead person can't die again. My brain, still processing the absurdity of being pushed through a door into an ancient Greek mythological world, couldn't decide if I was more terrified or confused. On the one hand, falling from the sky wasn't ideal. On the other hand, wait is that Mount Olympus in the distance?

I caught a glimpse of the rolling hills, sprawling vineyards, and rocky cliffs far below me, all bathed in the golden light of a Mediterranean afternoon. The smell of saltwater reached my nose, even as the wind whipped by me. I was falling fast, but, strangely, there was no sense of panic. Perhaps it was the "invincibility" gift, or perhaps my brain just couldn't figure out what was actually happening to me.

The free fall was taking longer than I had anticipated. I knew that early on I had tried screaming for a bit, but after the initial shock, I just stopped and began thinking logically. That's when the questions began. I just kept coming up with more questions until I realized that the ground was getting quite close.

"Oh well," I said, as I braced for whatever came next. "I guess I'll find out what invincibility is all about."

With a whoosh and a thud, I hit something soft then something very hard. The haystack exploded in all directions with splinters of hay shooting everywhere. Animals could gather around me in a fairly wide radius to munch on the hay and they'd hardly have to chew. If the horrendous collision didn't scare everything away, that is. I lay there for a moment, staring up at the clear blue sky, surrounded by the sweet, earthy smell of farmland. A cow somewhere nearby mooed disinterestedly which snapped me out of my stupor. I guess it hadn't been too scary for the livestock. I thought this after visually confirming the sound came from an unconcerned bovine who hadn't run away. She hadn't even stopped chewing or rechewing her meal. I saw the dispersed haystack that once had been just like one of its many counterparts that dotted the fields around me.

"Ah. Well. That was convenient," I muttered as I tried to sit up. I felt my muscles, young muscles at that, working smoothly for the first time in decades. I reveled in the sensation for a moment, stretching and flexing my arms.

"Well, would you look at that!" A voice, deep and jolly, rang out from somewhere nearby. My vision was still adjusting from the midday sun, but I could make out the silhouette of a large man approaching. He was wiping his hands on his dirty apron. Not an apron, he was wearing a tunic. "It's not every day the Mythics drop a visitor into my haystack. You all right there, young lady?"

I blinked and pulled myself up, picking bits of straw from my hair. The man who approached me was burly, with arms like tree trunks and a wide-brimmed hat that covered most of his sunburnt face. His nose was ruddy from sun exposure, and his beard was streaked with gray hairs. A friendly farmer, I guessed.

"Uh, I think so?" I replied, my voice more uncertain than my actual physical condition. I hadn't felt this limber for a long time. I actually felt great physically, it was the mentally I was more concerned about. "I'm...new here."

The man laughed heartily, his belly shaking beneath his tunic. "Aye, I reckon you are, falling out of the sky like that! Name's Daxeus, though most folks call me Dax." He gave a sweeping bow that seemed far too graceful for a man his size. "And you've landed right in the heart of the Pelasgos Valley. Finest farmland this side of the River Styx! Truth be told it's more of a strait than a river, but that's none of my business. The Mythics taught people what to call things and we do what we're told. They're not nearly as hospitable as we farmers, mind you."

My mind spun. "Pelasgos Valley? River Styx? Wait, this is actually Greece?"

Dax raised an eyebrow, looking me over with mild curiosity. "Uh, no. It's the Pelasgos Valley. If you mean to ask what the whole land is called, it's Neos Ellas. There's a big, painted map near the town square if you'd like a better understanding of the land. I can take you there once I round up the sheep you scared off with your less-than-graceful landing."

I finished brushing the last of the hay off my clothes. "So... I've landed in the middle of mythological farm country?"

"More or less!" Dax said with a wide grin, giving a sweep of his arm to the surrounding fields. "Beautiful, ain't it? Grows the best olives, figs, and grapes you'll ever taste! Though we've had a bit of a problem with the satyrs sneaking in and stealing the grapes. They are rascals, but what can you do?"

"Satyrs? Like, half-man, half-goat?" I asked, wide-eyed.

"Ah, don't let the hooves fool you," Dax said, waving a hand dismissively. "They're mostly harmless when they're not causing trouble. Some of them can even be helpful when they want to be. They enjoy eating some of the more annoying weeds that grow in with the crops. The problem is that sometimes they eat the crops too."

I mentally reminded myself that satyrs were probably not going to be the wildest thing I would see in this place and moved on with the conversation. "Dax, I don't know much about this place. If I help you round up your sheep, will you take me to the town square? I'd like to see that map you mentioned and get my bearings."

"I appreciate the offer, but my sheep will come when I call. It shouldn't be too long and I'll still take you to Melosia, that's the name of the town," said Dax, with a friendly smile. He seemed like a nice man and he made me feel a little less alone in this strange place. I hoped there were more people like him that were willing to help me get a plan together. The man in white was fairly vague about this whole process.

"Thank you, Dax. I guess I'll just sit for a moment and take in the sights." He nodded and I sat on the grass with my arms out behind me for support. Dax walked off and began to call for his flock to regroup.

I scanned my surroundings. There were fields and small farmhouses around me. Beyond that, I could see the tops of trees from the forest that lined the valley's edge. Some unknown number of miles past the tree line were beautiful mountain peaks. I'd only seen a small area of this place and I was already amazed at its picturesque landscape. I closed my eyes and enjoyed the warm sunlight on my face.

I was lost in the moment until I felt a tap on my footwear. I looked first at the leather sandals that I was evidently wearing and then followed a stave up to a smiling Dax.

"I'm sorry to wreck what was certainly a moment of relaxation, but I've got to get you to town if I want to return in time for dinner," said Dax. He had a small flock of sheep flocking about him.

"How many sheep do you have there?" I asked, with a devious smirk.

"Eighteen," said the unknowing victim of the stupid joke I was preparing.

"Dax, you have twenty sheep here," I said matter-of-factly. He adopted a confused face and quickly counted them.

"You must've hit harder than I thought. There's eighteen for certain." Dax raised an eyebrow in my direction as I prepared to spring the trap.

"I know, but I still wanted to help with your sheep, so I rounded them up," I said, delivering the stupid joke perfectly deadpan. Dax took a second, sighed, and then looked at me like a parent might look at a child who had filled out their math homework sheet with crayon drawings of stick figure animals.

"You either hit your head or you're just a bit off. Either way, let's get going, uh, I just realized that I never got your name," said Dax, pausing for a response. It wasn't just him pausing. It felt like everything paused. Even I paused. I realized that I couldn't move anything except for my eyes. I was close to having an issue with it when something else unexpected happened.

A golden hued rectangle popped into my field of vision. It was about arms length away from my face and moved with my vision so that it was always in the center of my eyeline. If I could've moved, I may have jumped back, but I was still frozen. I realized the box had text in it and read the single word question in my head. Name?

I couldn't speak out loud and couldn't move my arms to write down an answer, assuming a writing utensil was available. I realized that if I focused, I could keep the rectangle in place while still glancing past it or off to the side. My only limitation was how far my eyes could move without moving my face. I confirmed that everything around me had indeed frozen in place. One of the sheep had taken a bite of hay fragments and some had fallen out of its mouth. The gravity-refusing piece just hung there in midair.

I refocused on the text box and mentally thought my name at it as hard as I could. I felt a mental connection and 'Mae' appeared in the center of the floating rectangle. As soon as the name had been entered, the word 'confirm' presented itself on the bottom right corner of the rectangle. I mentally pushed the button and two things happened all at once. The world unfroze and the box disappeared.

"Mae? I don't think I've ever heard that name before," said Dax. I didn't remember actually saying my name out loud, but that was the least of my concerns.

"Did everything just freeze for you as well," I said, looking around with my now functional body. Dax just adopted a strange look again.

"Let's get you to Melosia. There is a good physician there and I am pretty sure that your humors are off," said Dax, raising more questions than answers.

He guided his sheep into a nearby pen with a few commands and secured the door. A boy in his mid teens ran up and stopped in front of Dax. The resemblance made it all too obvious they were related and the first word out of his mouth even more so.

"Father! I saw something falling from the sky from a distance and came running. Did it land nearby? Who's this woman? She looks confused," The boy said in quick succession.

"This is my son, Alexios," Dax said, turning to me. Then he turned back to his son. "Son, this confused woman is called Mae and she is what fell from the sky. I'm taking her to town to see Hippius. I think she hit her head very hard."

The boy's eye betrayed his feelings about everything his dad said as he glanced back and forth. "How did you survive?"

"I've been told that I've been given the gift of invincibility. Maybe that had something to do with it," I responded. The father and son looked at each other and back at me. After a few seconds of no one knowing what to say, Dax spoke.

"I wouldn't go around saying that, whether it's true or not. The Mythics don't like anything that can't be killed. Any threat to their power, real or imagined, and they'd spend every waking second figuring out their enemy's Achilles' elbow," said Dax with a worried expression.

"Achilles' heel?" I asked, correcting the now confused man.

"He couldn't heal from the damage to his elbow. It made him terrible in combat and he had to retire," Dax responded hastily.

"No, Achilles' heel. The bottom of his foot," I said, slightly flustered.

"I'm sure his foot could heal just fine. I honestly don't remember him hurting his foot in the story though," said Alexios, jumping in to help his dad. "Father, I think she did hit her head."

"Good thing it wasn't her elbow," said Dax. The two laughed at his terrible dad joke more than I thought was necessary. Although, to be fair, I thought no laughter was needed. I guess the man in white did say my adventure would inspired by ancient Greek mythology, not exactly the same. I wondered what else would be different as Dax wiped a tear from his eye when he was finished laughing. He waved for me to follow him.

I sighed and followed Dax as he weaved through a few fields. When we got to the edge of town, my excitement was renewed. The town was a maze of narrow, winding streets paved with worn stones. Their smooth surfaces told tales of centuries of footsteps. The houses were made of whitewashed stone, with terracotta-tiled roofs that sloped gently downwards. Many of the buildings had this modest, yet charming appearance. Ivy and flowering vines crawled up many walls around the wooden window frames. Small, round clay pots filled with fragrant herbs sat on windowsills, infusing the air with a pleasant aroma.

The heart of Melosia was its agora, a bustling square where people gathered to trade goods, share stories, and hear news. Market stalls lined the square, their vibrant awnings flapping in the wind. People were selling everything from freshly grown produce and warm, crusty bread to intricate jewelry and hand-spun wool. The air was filled with the chatter of merchants and the hum of negotiations, punctuated by the occasional clink of coins.

As we walked past one stall that had painted clay jars, I heard a sound like someone beckoning a cat. Slight movement caught my eye and it originated from one of the paintings on a jar. The head of one of the men beckoned me closer. I leaned in without thinking. Then, the painting spoke.

"Think about the word 'menu'," whispered the painted pottery. It must've noticed my confusion and repeated the request. Maybe I did need to see the doctor.

"I'm not hungry," I said, then continued following Dax through the busy square. As my mind continued processing, I had a realization. The painted man that spoke to me was dressed all in white and sounded like the man in white as well. I continued walking until we got to the large painted map.

"I'm going to go see if Hippius can see you. Wait here and try to get your bearings with the map. See if anything looks familiar," said Dax. Then, he went off into the crowd.

"Pssst," whispered the familiar voice. I looked around until I realized that the sound was coming from a bit of mosaic tile art on the wall bordering the map. "Think about the word 'menu' or even the word 'map'," said the voice, slightly louder this time.

"Fine," I said and I thought 'map'. Everything, including ambient sound paused all at once. A golden box filled my vision, but this time it had a perfect representation of the map I had just glanced at in perfect detail. I thought about the map going away and it did. The world unfroze in an instant when the map popped away. I experimented with the map a couple more times. I found that each time the map was present, the world around me stood still.

I was left standing there in the marketplace questioning what I was doing here and if this was even happening. "I think I do need to see a doctor after all."

Chapter 3

THE HUMORS

Dax returned soon after my map experiment had concluded. He was only slightly out of breath from the return jog. "I told Hippius about how you fell from the sky and landed on my farm. He'd like to see you immediately," said Dax, waving me to follow him.

"I think that's a good idea actually. I'm having the weirdest day," I said, not knowing how to explain further without sounding insane.

We hurried over to the doctor's office and I immediately understood the difference between ancient and modern medicine. This place looked more like an apothecary than a physician's office. There were plants everywhere, both live and dried, and various instruments for grinding or otherwise processing said plants. I saw a man who must've been about six feet tall. He had about one foot of white beard under a mostly bald head. Based on his height and Dax's, I figured that I must have kept my approximate height of around a five and a half feet tall. Hippius wore a white fabric tunic draped over his shoulders and a leather belt with a few pouches attached.

"Mae, it's nice to meet you. My name is Hippius and I'd like to try and help you, if I may," the man said in a voice that reminded me of a sweet old grandpa talking to his grandkids.

"That would be wonderful, although I will let you know in advance that I don't have any money," I said, with a bit of hesitation in my voice. I guessed that I was about to see how ancient medicine compared to modern in another aspect, billing practices.

"Don't worry about that, my dear. I heard your story and would be interested in helping with the only payment being an increase in knowledge," he said with a smile.

I told him about the fall, the time freezes, and the talking murals. He nodded along as I recounted the events, but his face grew more concerned over time. It reminded me of a time I took a city bus and sat next to a gentleman who explained to me, unbidden and in detail, about how birds didn't really exist. In this case, I was the bird denier though. It didn't feel great.

"If you would lay down here, Mae, I'd like to examine your head a bit," said Hippius. He then pointed to a simple wooden bench that was just big enough for a person to lie on with their legs hanging off the side from the knee down. I did as he asked and he began to poke and prod my head. Every once in a while a 'hmm' would escape his otherwise quiet inspection.

"Well, what do you see," I asked.

"Nothing out of the ordinary. Except for the fact that your head sustained no damage from the fall. Would you be okay with me administering a local anesthetic and attempting to use tools to find the answers we seek?" He asked. I just absentmindedly responded in the affirmative. If the ground couldn't hurt me, neither could he. I had my eyes closed as the ceiling wasn't any fun to look at anyway and I heard him shuffling around and grabbing tools.

I felt a force push me down the table and my body shot upward in response. My mouth dropped open when I turned to see him setting a fist-sized wooden mallet down amongst his tools. He grabbed a much larger wooden mallet and turned to me, surprised at my reaction.

"You may need a larger dose of the anesthesia," he said, then he shrugged at my lack of immediate response in the affirmative.

"First off, a hammer isn't an anesthetic. Second, it won't work anyway because I've been given the gift of invincibility," I said. Both of these statements were ones that I'd never imagine saying out loud.

"Remarkable," Hippius said, setting down the larger dose hammer. "I'd never dreamed that I'd be able to examine someone who was invincible! They don't usually need medical care after all."

"No more hammers though," I said. I felt myself smiling at the ridiculousness of it all.

Hippius turned back to his tools and grabbed the ancient equivalent of a scalpel and stepped toward me. "May I?"

I placed my arm out toward him out of sheer curiosity. If I was going to test out this invincibility, I might as well do it in a physician's office.

He gently put the edge of the blade to a spot on my arm. When nothing happened, he pushed a bit harder. The blade couldn't break the skin. There was no pain and the slight pressure wasn't uncomfortable. He smiled up at me like he had just opened exactly what he wanted on Christmas morning and I smiled back as the gift giver. He then proceeded to stab at me with the scalpel.

I instinctively raised a hand to block and the razor sharp point of the blade just gently pushed my hand back. I was sold. After all the physical pain I had experienced through my marriage and through my advanced age, this was the best power I could've gotten. I pushed away the negative memories and smiled back at Hippius.

"Do you have a sword by any chance?" I asked. He nodded excitedly and ran out of the room faster than I thought possible. He returned moments later with a beautiful bronze sword.

"I got this as a gift from the commander of an army that I assisted with healing decades ago. I've never had the need to wield it, but I think this is fitting," Hippius said excitedly.

I held out my arm and nodded for him to give it a good swing. He slashed down with all his might. When the sword hit my forearm, the energy transferred to my arm and it swung down and away. There was no damage and no pain. He looked at me expectantly and I gave him the verdict by twisting my arm around in front of him showing that no damage had been done. Further testing seemed unnecessary.

"Thank you for sharing this with me, Mae. I will keep it between us, so as not to arouse the anger of the Mythics and I think you should do the same. Next, I wanted to examine your humors," he said. He pulled out a book with text next to what appeared to be color samples from a local paint store that encompassed tones of every skin color I'd ever seen. "I'll just compare these colors with the color of your forearm and I should be able to get a good idea."

"I'm pretty sure that the humors aren't a thing anymore, but you do what makes you happy," I said, motioning him over. I remembered reading about ancient physicians who thought the different liquids in our bodies needed to be in balance along with other variations like elements or the seasons. That all got thrown out when humanity discovered germs and microorganisms though.

As he turned my forearm to examine a specific spot, the world paused again. I waited a moment to make sure he wasn't just holding his breath or something, but my inability to move confirmed it. A rectangle appeared in my vision once again, but this time it said 'Humors and Class selection'. There was a 'Continue?' option in the button right corner so I mentally pushed it.

A new page appeared and I read it a few times before selecting to continue. I had no idea what a class was and no idea how it would affect the rest of my time here. The finality of it really made me pause and think of all the ways I could mess up my time here by not taking this seriously.

You will now distribute your starting humor points and select a class based on your selections. Warning: Once you've confirmed your starting allocations and class, you will not be able to go back and make changes. As you grow in power, you will receive addi_ tional humor points, but your class will remain constant.

I mentally selected to continue. This whole part of my experience here felt so foreign, but having a map was always helpful. The ability to stop time also seemed like a superpower, but I wasn't going to look a gift horse in the mouth.

A new screen appeared. This one had a pie chart that was divided into four even sections. I read through the information given.

5 *Sanguin: This humor has a direct correlation to constitution and HP (Health Points).*

5 *Coleric: This humor has a direct correlation to speed and agility.*

5 *Flegmat: This humor has a direct correlation to intellect and luck.*

5 *Melanc: This humor has a direct correlation to strength and EP (Energy Points).*

Each of the four sections had a distinct color to its portion of the chart. Sanguin was red, Coleric was yellow, Flegmat was blue, and Melanc was gray. I guessed that these colors somehow told Hippius what my humors were, but all that really could've just been for show and I wouldn't have known any different. It didn't make sense to me as there were all sorts of skin tones and they didn't seem to match up with what the chart showed. I wasn't interested in figuring this part of the world out. I'd seen enough doctors in my long life and I didn't envy their job.

Each section had the number five as a starting point with a little plus and minus sign next to the number. I wasn't very interested in the first three humors and my reasoning seemed sound in my mind. I didn't need a lot of constitution as I am invincible. I didn't need to be all that fast for the same reason. My intellect seemed fine as I still had all of my wisdom from Earth. That left me with the humor of strength and energy, Melanc. These were two things that I had lacked most of my life, especially toward the end.

I had fourteen points to allocate as my starting pool and I put them all into Melanc. I mentally pushed the button to confirm my selections. The pie chart updated to show the Melanc humor as over half of the circle. A new screen appeared.

> *Based on your allocations, there is only one option available for class specialization.*
> *You have defaulted to the Kolossos class.*

I only had myself to blame for the lack of choices. I wasn't overly upset. I didn't even really know what kind of effect class would have on me and I was still invincible anyway. I mentally pushed the button to confirm my class selection. Time resumed and the tall bench I was sitting on creaked. Hippius was still staring at my forearm very closely. Only the second creak from the bench broke his attention. When the bench cracked and sent me crashing to the floor, his attention was fully broken.

He scrambled to get me up off of the ground and that's when we both had a realization. He had already begun to speak at this point. "Your humors are imbalanced and lean heavily Melanc," he gulped and cleared his throat as I stood to my full height. "You've grown."

"Sorry about your bench," I said in surprise. I was now slightly looking down on the man. As I was looking at him I noticed two static bars at the bottom left of my vision. One was red and one was green. I'd have to figure that out later as I was beginning to feel overwhelmed.

"It is of no concern to me. I can rebuild it. What just happened to you though?" He asked. On impulse he grabbed my forearm and then my bicep. "How did you just put on so much muscle?"

"I don't know," I said, starting to panic a little more. I hadn't noticed the extra muscle until he started feeling my arm. I pulled the fabric of my tunic up a little. My calves were huge. "I don't know!"

After a moment of awed silence, I was starting to feel slightly claustrophobic in the room. It was as if the room had shrunk on me and not the other way around.

"Just take a few deep breaths and calm yourself down. Everything will be okay," said Hippius in his kind, old man voice. He could see my anxiety and panic setting in.

"I need some air," I said, moving to the door that I felt like I had to duck through, but I probably wouldn't have hit my head. Not that it mattered. I could hit my head as hard as anyone had ever hit a head and I would've been fine. I stepped out into the bustling town square. Someone bumped into me and I spun away as they apologized. I lost my footing and caught myself on the building. I wasn't used to this larger body.

I turned and took a few steps to get acclimated. As the steps came more quickly I smiled at the power I was feeling. The clumsiness, not so much. I almost stepped on a cat, but was able to pivot at the last moment. Unfortunately, I pivoted right into a stall that was selling rugs. I caught myself, but I knocked a half dozen rugs out of place. The stall owner asked me if I was okay, but my head was spinning and I was overwhelmed.

I squatted down and covered my ears as more people gathered to help pick up the rugs and check to see if I was okay. The cacophony of voices and other ambient noises from the market overloaded my systems. I needed to get out of there as soon as possible. My legs exploded with power and I leapt up into the air far above the tallest building in Melosia. I landed on a roof near the edge of town and looked back toward the town square. I had probably just jumped close to a football field in length and I really wanted to do it again.

I squatted for another jump, hoping to land just outside of town this time. The roof that had already taken the brunt of my landing couldn't also handle a takeoff. I crashed through the flat roof of the single-story building and looked around quickly. No one was home and based on the dust and cobwebs, no one would be home anytime soon.

Still overwhelmed by the new class, powers, and location. I laid down on a nearby bed and decided it was time for a nap. My flight or fight response had triggered some sleepiness and I was thankful for the quiet breather.

Chapter 4

PRETTY JUMPY

I saw my late husband in a dream that felt like it was real. He was young and smiling at me. This was before we were married. I remembered the suit he was wearing. He wore it to our first date. It was an ill-fitting, hand-me-down suit, but I didn't care. We got along so well and I thought he was handsome anyway. He was so funny and he loved that I would make cheeky comments that most other ladies in our graduating class wouldn't dare make. It was such a fond memory, but it didn't last.

A hard knock resounded from the front door and I startled awake.

"Is there anyone in there? This is the city guard," said a loud and strong voice. I sat up and thought through my options. I could answer and try to explain the hole in the roof and my being in someone else's home in the first place or maybe I just wait and see if they leave. A few moments passed before the voice continued. "This is the city guard. If no one answers we will have to enter by force."

"So much for them just going away," I said to myself. Looks like I'm either talking with them or leaping out of the hole in the roof. The opening was only about ten feet up so I knew that I could easily hop out of this situation.

A man poked his head over the edge of the ceiling hole and saw me standing below him. I figured him for another guard from his goofy helmet. Either that or he liked to sweep floors while walking on his hands. The bronze helmet had a bright red mohawk.

"Are you okay, miss? Could you please open the door for the other guard?" Asked the roof guard. I wasn't good at refusing authority figures' polite requests, so I did as he asked and went to the door. I heard his retreating footsteps as he descended from the roof and joined his partner at the front door.

Moments later, both guards were inside the house with me. They had taken a step back at first upon seeing my size and muscles, but soon remembered their duty. The roof guard spoke first.

"Miss, we received a complaint of a loud crash at this residence. Are you hurt?" He asked. He was very kind and the care in his voice was in stark contrast to his intimidating arms and armor.

"I'm fine, thank you. I fell through the roof. I'm sure that was the noise that was reported. I appreciate you checking on me," I said, purposefully being vague. I moved slightly toward the door to encourage them to leave. They didn't budge.

"I've never seen you around town before. Is this your house?" Asked the door guard who must've been the bad cop in this scenario. His voice was a little more gruff.

"I've not been here before. I dropped in on a local farmer and he was nice enough to bring me to town for a visit," I said, not technically lying. I moved again. They didn't again.

"So, this isn't your house. Why were you on the roof?" Bad cop asked. It was a completely logical line of questioning.

"We are just trying to get to the bottom of this and ensure the city's safety. Would you please answer his question of why you were on the roof?" Asked the good cop guard.

"I don't have a good reason. I just kind of landed there. I can promise you that I wasn't doing anything malicious," I answered honestly. The guards looked at each other. Bad cop guard smiled a bit and good cop guard looked a little sad.

"We're going to have to take you to the captain of the guard. Come with us," said the gruffer of the two. They took a step toward me and I felt myself going into fight or flight mode again. I did the first thing that popped into my head. My map opened. Time froze.

The guards stood there motionless. I was thankful for the extra time to think. I calmed myself and weighed my options. I could still jump out of the roof hole. I could possibly overpower the guards and escape. Or I could just go with them and hope I don't get thrown in prison or something. I wasn't going to risk the last option and really didn't want to fight these guards and make things worse. This left me with one option.

I unfroze everything and took a few quick steps back from the guards.

"Wait up fellas, I think I dropped a better answer to your last question on the ground over there," I said, positioning myself under the hole. They looked at each other again, but this time it was out of confusion. It gave me the few extra seconds I needed to squat down and pretend to look for something on the floor. I focused my power into my legs and pushed off as hard as I could. I jumped at a slight angle to hopefully land outside of the city.

In a flash, I was high above the rooftops again. I wished that I could see the looks on those guards' faces, but I was relieved to be out of the situation. I pulled up my map again and my body froze in midair. I squinted mentally trying to get a closer view of the landscape surrounding the city. To my surprise, the map zoomed in and I realized that it naturally centered on a small arrowhead that was pointing to the west of the city. That must be my location and the direction that I was facing. This interactive map was incredible. I took note of my current location and then popped my map away. After a few seconds, I pulled the map back up and confirmed my heading. I was facing west, but moving east as I had been angled slightly back when I jumped. Based on how far up I was and how much I moved in those brief seconds, I could get a pretty good idea of where I would land. East of Melosia stood a few foothills. I figured that I could hop to the opposite side of the nearest hill and then head south to the next town. My goal was to not almost get arrested there.

I felt a little bad for not saying goodbye to Hippius or Dax, but hopefully after a bit of time I can go back and the heat will be off. It was early afternoon by my estimation, if the sun and time works the same way here. I'd need a few hours to build a simple lean-to, a fire, and try to find something to eat. The map showed a river to the south that fed into a lake. If I follow the river I'm sure I'll find fresh water and food. Luckily, I'd taken David camping often enough to develop some outdoors skills.

I started thinking about my son, David. He would beg me to go camping almost every weekend when he was younger. I wasn't sure if he wanted to go because he enjoyed it or if he just wanted to get away from his father. It was probably both. I know I enjoyed the peace of the great outdoors, but I also enjoyed the time away. My husband died years ago, but the feelings still flooded back. I stopped that line of thinking and focused on the present. One thing was sure in my mind and it was that the issues I had with my husband weren't going to follow me here.

After another jump and a short run where I didn't get winded while going faster than I remember ever running, I found the river. The surrounding forest provided everything I needed for the shelter and campfire. On Earth, water and food would've been my next priorities, but I hadn't eaten or drank anything since I arrived and I wasn't hungry or thirsty. Maybe I didn't need to worry about food and water here. I thought back to the town square and the market stalls. There were definitely stalls that sold food items and produce. I figured that a test would be helpful to get some answers.

I walked over to the river that I'd set up my camp near. I stepped into the river and stood there in water that was about waist high. I stood perfectly still and waited to see if a fish would swim by. After a few minutes, a decent sized fish came near enough for me to make a grab for it. It wasn't like I had a net or fishing pole, so this was my bright idea. I wasn't quick enough for the fish and it swam away. I regretted not putting any points into the attribute that would've given me more speed.

I tried a couple more times and after the last miss I smacked the water with all of my strength in frustration. I fish that I hadn't even seen floated to the surface. It turned out that he was only stunned momentarily as he swam away before I could reach him. It was enough to give me an idea. I waited a few minutes to allow time for any nearby fish to acclimate to my presence again. Then, I smacked down on the water's surface as hard as I could. This was overkill as water splashed out in giant arcs from where my palms hit the water. I was able to locate a stunned fish and smacked its head on a rock to dispatch it as humanely as possible.

A notification popped up in the top left of my vision, but only stayed briefly. I was so surprised and confused by it that I didn't read it fully. I only knew that it had said something about defeating a fish. That was odd. I decided to just go back to my campfire and continue my testing. I used a stick to skewer the fish and placed it over the fire for cooking.

The sun was beginning to set as I broke the now cooked fish open and tried eating some of it. Nothing seemed to change. I wasn't sure what I was expecting. I wasn't hungry in the first place, so I wasn't feeling satiated or as if a need was met. I sat next to the fire, staring at the fish that I didn't really have a desire to eat, but I didn't want to waste it either. I kind of felt bad for smacking it in the first place.

"What do I do now?" I said, looking up in the general direction of where I fell from. I guess I was asking the man in white, but I wasn't expecting an answer.

"Who?" Asked a voice from somewhere in the darkening forest behind me. The sun was down far enough to make the fire a necessity at this point. I looked out toward the trees and squinted for a better look. I saw nothing.

"Who's there?" I asked, a little louder this time. I got to my feet and into a defensive position.

"Who?" Repeated the mysterious voice.

"That's what I'm asking. Who are you? Show yourself," I was still focusing on the trees when I caught movement. It was higher up than I had expected and it scared me a little.

An owl landed on the ground near the fire and eyed the fish that still had a good amount of meat on it. "Who?" Screeched the owl. I relaxed a bit when I saw that there wasn't a threat.

"You can have the fish. That would actually help me feel a little better about killing it for no reason," I said motioning to the fish and sitting back down as if this was a normal occurrence.

"Who?" The owl repeated for a now unacceptable number of times.

"Could you stop saying who?" I asked the owl as it took a tentative step toward the fish.

"I apologize," said the owl. "Although that is a normal noise for an owl to make. Perfectly normal."

I crawled backward away from the bird after a small jolt.

"You're pretty jumpy for someone with invincibility," said the owl with an unnatural looking tilt of its head. "I'm here to help you, Mae."

The bird knowing my name hadn't taken away my trepidation. The more I processed though, the more I thought that this must be one of the helpers that the man in white had set up for me.

The owl took another step, pulled the fish down from it's skewer, and began eating. I watched while still processing the situation as it finished its meal and then looked up at me. The awkward silence stretched out a bit too long for comfort.

"Thank you for the fish. My name is Noctua and I'm here to provide you with some help. I've been given a decent amount of information about this place and a little about you. I will answer any questions you have to the best of my ability," said the owl, which then took a moment to clean off a few feathers before approaching me.

"I have a decent amount of questions, but I also don't know what I don't know," I said. I got comfortable in front of the fire and thought through what to ask first. I'd seen and experienced too much to question a talking owl.

"The only true wisdom is in knowing you know nothing," said Noctua. "Although, you do know quite a lot from your decently long life. It's good that you are showing humility and acknowledging that there is much you can learn. I think I will be able to help you quite a bit."

"Am I speaking with an owl that just quoted Socrates?" I asked, rhetorically to myself. I pinched myself to make sure that I was awake. I didn't feel any pain, so it didn't help with confirmation.

"You sure are," said Noctua. She hopped toward me and did the crazy head tilt that owls do. I wasn't a huge fan of the move, but somehow it helped me to get out of my own head and understand that this owl was here to help. I wasn't about to waste the opportunity to get answers.

"Okay, well I guess my first question would be. Why am I here exactly?"

Chapter 5

Good Night

"I could tell you that you are here by this campfire because you built it and it brings a sense of comfort to you. I could tell you that you are out here in the wilderness because you were feeling overwhelmed in Melosia and your flight response took over. I could tell you that you are here in an ancient Greek inspired world because when you were on Earth your flight response often took you to ancient Greek worlds. Those trips were through books, but the desire to escape was the same," stated the owl in a pragmatic way.

"So, I am here to escape?" I asked. Her words hit me hard, so the question came out more defensive than I had intended.

"In a way, although escape isn't the best word for what you are needing to accomplish here. True freedom will come when you learn what you need to learn and face what you need to face," said Noctua.

"I'm feeling pretty free at the moment," I said with a hint of sass.

"Camping and temporarily comforting yourself may feel like freedom, but it is fleeting. Soon you will begin to revisit more difficult moments from life on Earth while you sleep. This has been deemed the safest way for you to revisit those memories which is to your benefit for healing. They will remind you of what triggered your flight response, there and here. Remember, understanding yourself and the trauma of your past will help paint a more complete picture. Think on this and rest. I will return." The owl flew into a nearby tree and left me alone by the fire. I stared into the flickering flames and thought about what she had said.

"This obviously has something to do with the main reason for wanting to run away in my life," I said while staring into the fire. I didn't know if the owl could hear me, but I felt it may help to brainstorm out loud anyway. I didn't really want to think about my husband, but based on the brief glimpse I had had of him when I briefly fell asleep after my first big jump, it seemed inevitable. The memory was of him on our first date. I fell in love with that man so quickly and we had a good relationship before the war. He had come back a shadow of his former self, but I wouldn't fully realize that fact for a couple years. David was born about a year after his father came home. He never met the man I fell in love with.

I shook my head and clenched my fists. "No," I said with anger boiling up in me. "I'm not here to think about that man. This place is like a paradise to me and I'm going to enjoy it." I sat watching the fire until I began to get drowsy then I laid under the simple shelter I had made and drifted off to sleep. I had the same weird vision as before which replayed my first date with my late husband. This part of my story was overtly positive, but it brought the contrast of what he would become into focus. The Dr. Jekyll and Mr. Hyde-esque man was definitely what I'd been trying to escape. The dream was actually a nightmare, just like much of my marriage had been.

The vision ended with me leaning in for a good-night kiss and him pecking me on the cheek gently and respectfully. I woke up to an involuntary kick of my leg. No, it wasn't a kick and it wasn't involuntary. A lion had my shin in his mouth and had given it a sudden jerk. If I wasn't invincible the lion may have torn my leg clean off. I sat up, surprisingly calm in the situation, and smacked at the lion's forehead as if I was swatting a house cat away from some food that they weren't supposed to have. The swing didn't connect. I hadn't meant it too. It was a warning.

The lack of pain and the fact that my leg was absolutely fine, provided me with a sense of security in the gift I had been given. As if falling from the sky and the attempted stabbing wasn't enough, a lion was biting my leg and doing no damage. I found myself smiling.

I wiggled my leg with all my might and the lion's head shook along with it, but he held firm. It was like playing tug-of-war with a dog.

"Enough!" I shouted. There was a good amount of power in my voice, but the lion ignored me. All the anger that I had felt at seeing my dead husband's face again welled up inside of me. This was a very unfortunate turn of events for the lion. I brought my non-grappled leg away from the big cat and gave it a mighty swing towards its head. My leg connected and the lion's jaw immediately went limp. I extracted my leg from the dazed lion's mouth and stood to face it. I realized that I was happier now than I had felt in decades, maybe ever. I was powerful and I wasn't a victim. I showed the lion my true power as if I was showing my late husband.

The lion was able to shake off the effects of the first strike and leapt toward me. I wasn't fast, but I could punch a lion who was helpless to dodge in mid-air. I didn't hold back. The haymaker connected with the lion's shoulder as its claws reached my torso. The claws did nothing, but the punch was devastating. The lion flew in the direction of the force and rag-dolled into a tree with a sickening thunk. It flopped to the ground, unmoving.

The notification about defeating a lion popped up and disappeared before I could focus on it. I'd have to ask Noctua about the messages and probably about the class selection process as well. I was guessing that I'd have to wait until closer to nightfall as owls were nocturnal creatures, but it would be worth it to get some more information. For now, I'd gotten a taste of true power, so of course I wanted more of that feeling. I couldn't punch my late husband, but I could punch a monster or two. There had to be monsters here after all, with this place being based on ancient Greek mythology. Mythology is lousy with monsters. I looked at my map to get a heading.

I was close to Lake Narcis, which gave me a chuckle when I got the joke. At least, I thought it might be a joke from the man in white. The character named Narcissus in Greek mythology fell in love with his reflection from a pool of water. Were the goofy, ancient Greek mythology puns and references going to be a recurring theme? I was personally all for it. I refocused and thought that if I ran the whole way, and maybe did some jumping, I figured that I could make it to Thermos by nightfall. Someone in that town had to know where some monsters were.

The trip was disappointingly dull on the monster front, but the beauty of the landscape that I passed was incredible. The lake had been picturesque with it reflecting the mountain peaks in the distance and the trees of the surrounding forest. It looked like something my favorite public broadcasting station artist would paint.

Past the lake was miles and miles of thick forest. My clothing was taking a beating from the passing branches and trees, some of which snapped as I hit them mid jump. By the time I was on the outskirts of Thermos, my clothes looked like I'd had a fight with a lawnmower. Maybe someone would let me do some work for a fresh set.

The guard on a lookout platform above the northern gate shouted out as I approached. "Who goes there?"

"My name is Mae. I'm just a traveler and I have no weapons," I said, loud enough for him to hear.

"Approach, traveler," the guard said. He came through the gate and rested the spear he was holding into the crook of his arm and motioned me to come closer. I walked over and gave him a dainty wave. It didn't match my intimidating form and he cracked a smile at the oddness of what he was seeing.

"You look like you just fought in an arena without armor or something," said the guard as he looked me over.

"I fought a big lion. Does that count?" I asked.

"I believe it does. Were you injured at all?" Asked the guard. I thought about my invincibility, but resolved not to say anything about it here.

"I must've gotten lucky," I said, shaking my head in the negative. "He tried to hurt me though."

"If you're up for another test of your strength, I think the town elders may have a task that would be perfect for someone of your, uh, stature," he smiled up at me as he finished his sentence. I was almost a full foot taller than him and about twice as wide with muscle.

"Thanks, I'll look into it. Is there somewhere I could stay for the night?" I asked. I may not have felt pain, but there was still fatigue. I had used my new muscles a lot to get here quickly.

"Of course," he turned and pointed toward what ended up being the main path through town. "Just follow this main road until you see some shops, then turn right and you'll see a sign that says 'The Golden Hearth'. They should have a room for you."

"Thank you," I said. He nodded at me in reply and continued his guard duty after letting me through.

The inn was easy enough to find. The couple of shops I passed were closed, but I didn't have any money yet anyway so I wasn't too worried about visiting them. As I entered the inn, a woman who looked to be in her forties smiled up at me and excitedly waved me over to the counter she had been leaning on.

"Come in from the wilderness, dear. How can I help you?" She asked sweetly. As I approached she gasped and ran around the counter to get to me. "What happened to you, poor thing?"

"Just a little lion attack, I'm okay," I said, as if that was a normal occurrence. She looked surprised, but then her motherly instincts kicked in and she ran off again just as fast. She was only out of sight for a few minutes and came back with a folded cloth under one arm.

"Put this on dear," she said, handing me what I now knew was a fresh tunic. I took the clothes, thanked her, and looked around for a place to change. "Come with me, we've got an empty room doing no one any good. Are you hungry?"

I followed her to the room after assuring her that I didn't need anything at the moment. I actually didn't know why I wasn't hungry or thirsty. I had a quick thought to inform her of my situation.

"You're being very kind, but I feel that I must tell you something before you help me. I don't have any money right now, but I'm a hard worker and would be willing to do some chores or something to pay you," I said. Even as I was trying to get the words out she was already waving them away.

"Don't you worry about that right now. Why don't you get some sleep and we'll work everything out in the morning?" She asked it as a question, but I felt like I was being instructed more than asked. She was a sweet woman and I wasn't about to question her kindness.

"Yes, ma'am," I said, remembering my manners and that I was younger than her in this world.

"Good night, dear." She closed the door and I was once again alone with my thoughts. I changed and sat on the surprisingly comfortable bed. I laid down and thought about the lion attack and how good it felt to have the strength to defend myself. There was an odd comfort to it. I fell asleep and into an intense nightmare. It felt so real, like it was happening to me. I quickly realized that what I was experiencing was from Felix's point of view.

One day I was working in the shop, fixing carburetors as usual, and the next thing I knew, I had a letter in my hand telling me I was off to train as a gunner in a bomber crew. I had a young woman who had just become my wife and I was all set for the American dream. How could this happen? I wouldn't even be able to enjoy settling into married life before they shipped me out. I told myself I'd be back soon and we could live out our fairytale together. That's what I promised her when I kissed her goodbye at the station.

The training was quick. We were taught how to man the guns, how to identify enemy fighters, and how to keep calm under pressure. I wasn't prepared. None of us were. But we learned fast, or we were humiliated and punished by the men training us. Our first mission was over enemy territory, a bombing run on a factory. I remember the way my hands shook when I climbed into that metal belly for the first time, the cold biting through my gloves. You couldn't talk much once you were up there; the engines were too loud. We had headsets, but mostly we just sat in silence, each of us lost in our own thoughts. Dreaming of being home, or anywhere else.

The first time we got hit, it didn't feel real. There was this sudden jolt, like we'd hit a pothole in the sky, and then I heard someone yell over the radio, "We've lost the tail!" I turned and saw the damage. Flames were licking up the back of the plane, smoke pouring out, and the tail gunner's station was just gone. Danny was back there. He'd been talking about his high school sweetheart that morning, showing us her picture. Now he was gone, just like that. I was almost nineteen, and I'd seen death for the first time. I thought I'd throw up, but I didn't. I just stared at where he used to be thinking about how that could've been me. Thinking about how I may never see my high school sweetheart again.

We made it back, but it wasn't a victory. I saw the way the other crews looked at us when we landed, the way their eyes avoided ours, like we were dead men walking. They told us to rest up and be ready for the next mission, like we hadn't just lost a friend. Like it was nothing. I didn't sleep that night. I just lay there, listening to the engines start up again and again in my head, that or Danny's voice.

The next mission was worse. More flak, more enemy fighters. You'd see them coming out of the clouds, black shadows darting across the sky, and then the tracers, bright and deadly, streaking towards you. We were supposed to keep our cool. Keep our heads down and our fingers on the triggers, but how do you do that when everything around you is exploding, and you know any second you could be next? We lost two more from our squad that day. I saw one of the bombers go down, the wings breaking off, and I thought about the guys in there, how they must have been screaming, praying, crying. I was numb. That's the only way I got through it. I just shut it all down.

I couldn't keep it shut down forever. They sent us up again and again. Every time we lost more of ourselves, whether physically or just mentally. By the time they called me back for a short leave, I didn't even know who I was anymore. I went home and my wife was there. She was smiling and so happy to see me, but I couldn't smile back. I felt like a ghost, like I was walking through my own life, watching it from the outside.

She asked me if I was okay, and I just said I was tired. That's all I could say if I could say anything. How do you tell your loved ones that every time you close your eyes, you see your friends dying? That you can still hear the way they screamed when the plane was hit, that you feel guilty for being alive? So most of the time I was silent. I turned to other things, hoping to dull the pain and silence the noise. When that didn't work, I got more and more angry, but this was pushed down deep too.

I was back up in the air a week later. New crew, new faces. They looked at me like I was some kind of veteran, someone who'd been through it and come out the other side, but I felt like a fraud. I didn't want to know their names. I didn't want to hear about their lives back home, because I knew what was going to happen. And I was right. We got hit bad. One of the engines blew, and we started to spiral. I remember grabbing onto the gun, trying to brace myself, and just praying that it would be quick. But it wasn't quick. The new guys, the ones who had looked up to me, got torn apart by shrapnel and bullets. I made it out, again, somehow only taking a single shot through the meat of my right leg. I crawled away from the wreckage, rolled into some nearby foliage, and passed out. I guess it was just human nature to try and survive, but the hope of a happy life had disappeared months ago.

I had fleeting moments of lucidity where I heard German soldiers and gunshots, but none of the bullets were aimed at me. I was safe in my hiding place. The next thing I remembered was waking up in a field hospital. They said some GIs found me when they searched the area where the bomber went down. They said I was lucky, but I didn't feel lucky.

When I got back home, after a while in hospital and a purple heart that I couldn't stand to look at. I could tell something was wrong. I hadn't healed. My wife would try to talk to me, but I didn't want to talk. I didn't want anything. About a year into civilian life and I had a son. It was all a blur. Maybe it was survivor's guilt or stress from the trauma that told me I didn't deserve this. I wanted to be a good father, but I didn't know how to be anything but angry anymore. Angry and scared, a vicious cycle.

One night, Mae asked me about the war and about getting help. I snapped. I yelled at her, called her terrible things, and told her she didn't understand. She tried to calm me down, but I couldn't stop. My physical treatment of her was my biggest regret. She didn't deserve this angry, violent monster's outbursts.

From that day forward, I saw the fear in her eyes, and it was like a punch to the gut every time. I'd brought the war home with me, and now I was hurting the people that I loved most. But even then, I couldn't change. The anger, the guilt, the nightma res... they didn't go away. I'd wake up in the middle of the night, drenched in sweat, and I'd hear my son crying in the next room, and I'd just want to scream.

She had said there were counselors, people who could help, but how could I talk to them? How could I sit there and tell someone who hadn't experienced any of it about the things I'd seen, the things I'd done. I couldn't even talk to my own wife? So I didn't go. I just kept it all inside and it ate me alive. I'd lash out, throw things, break things, and my wife would just stand there, trying to hold it together, trying to be strong for our son, but I could see it was killing her too.

I was a broken man, a monster who hurt people because he doesn't know how to do anything else. I didn't want to be this way, but I didn't know how to stop. The war didn't end when I left the skies. It followed me home, and now it's inside me, like a darkness I can't shake, a storm that won't pass. And I'm afraid, so afraid, that one day I'll die without telling my wife how sorry I was. Not that it would change anything. I already knew where I was going when I died.

The nightmare ended as suddenly as it had begun. I jolted up in the bed and looked around the otherwise empty inn room. Early morning light was streaming in through the window. I'd never felt so many feelings during and after a nightmare. It felt so real. I felt everything that he had felt. The worst part about the whole horrible ordeal was that as I processed what I had just seen, I understood something that I'd never known from a perspective that I could've never imagined.

I'd just seen and felt what my late husband had experienced from the time he was drafted to the first few years after he returned home. Felix had never told me that whole story. I guess it was another gift from the man in white. I did have a strange sense of closure in having the answer to a question that had bothered me for decades. The nightmare gave me something else though as well. The embers of anger that had been in me, long smothered by feelings of powerlessness and doubt had grown into an inferno.

I felt no sympathy for the monster my husband had become and I felt no sympathy for whatever monster I faced next in this world. Whatever it was going to be. It was going to feel my wrath.

Chapter 6

ONE DRACHMA

I walked out of my room and back to the great room of the inn. The innkeeper saw me and walked over to me with a big smile on her face.

"Good morning!" She said with excitement in her voice. "You're looking well rested. I've got a deal to discuss with you if you're up for it."

"Absolutely," I said, desperate for a distraction and to be thinking about anything other than my late husband.

"Well, I thought of a way for you to pay for the room and earn a little extra coin as well," said the innkeeper. I realized that I'd never asked for her name and felt a little rude.

"I'll do whatever I can to repay your kindness. I'm sorry to say, but I don't know your name," I said.

"My name is Xenia and what's your name, dear?" The sweet woman asked.

"My name is Mae," I said. Xenia pointed me to a table and I sat.

"Why don't you have a little bite to eat and then you can go out and help my husband load up some logs that he needs to deliver today?" She hurried back to the kitchen and brought out a bowl of stew and a piece of bread that looked to have been ripped off a much bigger loaf.

"Thank you. Loading logs sounds just fine." I ate the food she had provided even though I still wasn't feeling all that hungry. I still didn't quite understand when I was supposed to eat here, but my body must need fuel. I decided to worry about this question later and just focus on the task at hand. I needed to load logs and then I needed to punch something very hard.

We walked to a building on the outskirts of town that ended up being the innkeeper's house. It was right up next to the forest and had its own gate built into the town wall. A man came up to meet us as we approached and he hugged Xenia. He was a muscular man and a similar build to my own.

"Mae, this is my husband, Heracles. If you could help him load all of the logs that need to be loaded, we'll pay you a drachma. The stay at the inn is an obol, but we can worry about that next time. I've got to get back to the inn so I'll leave you to it," said

Xenia. Then she quickly headed back to The Golden Hearth.

"Thank you for helping me out, Mae. The loading part usually would take me the better part of a day if I have to load the cart by myself," said Heracles.

"I'm glad to help. Your wife is a very sweet woman. She gave me clothing and a place to sleep even though I had no money," I said. He nodded and waved for me to follow him. There was a not-so-hidden smile when I spoke of his wife. We walked to a large stack of logs that had been cut to about ten foot lengths. I had no idea what a log that size weighed, but it didn't look light. He pointed to one end of the first log and I moved into position. We each took an end and lifted the log to about waist high. After walking the log over to the cart, he struggled to lift the log high enough to clear the side of the cart.

"See what I mean, those logs are a beast. It's a good workout though, don't you think?" He said, still working on catching his breath. I wasn't winded at all though and honestly it didn't feel all that heavy. I wanted to try an experiment.

"Heracles, would you mind if I tried to lift one of those logs by myself?" I asked. He raised an eyebrow, but nodded that it was fine with him.

I walked over to the next log and squatted down to get my arms underneath it. I stood to my full height, with the log coming along for the ride. I could feel Heracles' eyes on me as I hefted the log onto one shoulder with a smooth motion. The weight, though substantial, felt manageable in my grasp, far lighter than I expected. There was a strange satisfaction in feeling this powerful, in knowing what my body was capable of.

I turned and walked the log over to the cart, hoisting it up and dropped it in place with a deep thud. Heracles whistled softly, clearly impressed. He shook his head and let out a breathy laugh.

"Well, I'll be. You've got more strength in you than I gave you credit for," he said, his hands on his hips as he watched me. "I'd have to hire multiple helpers from the village to get my work done that quickly."

I shrugged, a small smile pulling at the corner of my mouth despite myself. "I guess I'm full of surprises."

We spent the next couple of hours in relative silence, loading log after log into the cart. Heracles was a hard worker and, though we didn't speak much, there was an ease to the work. A rhythm. I felt grounded for the first time in a long time, focused on the physical labor and not the storm of thoughts that clouded my mind. I managed to not think about Felix the whole time.

When the last log was loaded, Heracles dusted off his hands and looked at me with a grin. "That went faster than I expected, thanks to you. Xenia and I owe you more than just a drachma."

"One drachma is fine," I said quickly, wanting to refuse any more charity. "I told you that I was happy to help. Xenia showed me kindness in giving me the replacement clothing and a room for the night."

"Still, you've earned my respect today, Mae. Not just anyone can do what you just did." He reached into his pocket and handed me the drachma with a firm nod. "If you're ever in need of work again, don't hesitate to come find me."

The coin was slightly smaller than a quarter. It was silver and had engravings on the front and back, although I only looked briefly as I didn't want him to think I was questioning his payment. I went to pocket the coin, but as soon as I thought about putting it away, it popped out of my hand and a notification popped up that simply said '1 drachma'. I thought about pulling the coin back out and it popped into my hand again. It was the weirdest feeling when the coin disappeared. I guess this is how money worked here although I didn't know how much exactly a drachma was. I'd have to ask someone and see what

I could figure out. Also, how many obols were in a drachma?

I gave Heracles a small wave, and made my way back into the town. The day was still early, the sun sitting high in the sky, casting long shadows from the rooftops of the modest buildings. I needed to find the town elders that the guard had mentioned and ask about the task that needed doing. The guard made it sound like maybe it was another beast of some sort, but I wouldn't know for sure until I found them.

I headed toward the town square, where I figured the leaders would be or where I could ask for directions. The square was lively with townsfolk going about their day. Merchants were selling from stalls, children were running after each other, and laughter echoed between the buildings. It felt surreal to walk among them, knowing that this place was not fully real. What did the man in white say? Something like an in-between place before moving to your eternal destination. I wasn't about to figure it out now, but maybe I could ask the owl the next time I saw her. I hoped that it would be soon because the amount of questions that were bouncing around my brain were multiplying.

I found the town elders seated at a stone bench near a fountain. I guessed that they just sat there to ensure everything went smoothly with the town, or they just wanted to be present if needed. Their presence was commanding, yet calm. It was a stark contrast to the chaos I often carried within me. Their sharp eyes found mine as I approached.

"You must be Mae," the central one said, his voice deep and steady. "A town guard and our local innkeeper told us about you. I guess you made quick work of loading Heracles' cart."

"Yes, I'm Mae," I replied, standing before them. This place had that small town bonus of everyone knowing everything. "And I'm here because I've been told there's a task that needs doing. I've come to offer my help."

The central elder nodded slowly, folding his hands in his lap. "You've heard correctly. It's a creature from the old world, one that's wandered too close to our borders. This monster has been driving people from their farms, attacking livestock, and putting everyone here on edge. If you're truly offering your help, we could certainly use it."

Another of the elders spoke, he wore glasses and had been reading a book when I approached. He sounded extremely thoughtful of his word choice. As if each word was precious and he didn't want to waste them. "Based on the description given by the survivors, I'd say this creature is an ophiotaurus."

I scanned my knowledge bank of Ancient Greek mythology, but remembered nothing with that name. "I'm sorry sir, I'm not familiar with that creature. Could you elaborate?"

"An ophiotaurus is a monster with the front half of a bull and the back half of a slithering serpent. It's larger than any naturally occurring bull as it has lived for many generations. None of the tales I've read about them speak of someone facing one in combat and living," said the bespectacled elder.

I could feel the weight of his words settle in my chest, but there was no hesitation in my response. "I'm ready." I was surprised at how agreeable I was with knowingly walking into danger. I'd never felt that way my entire life. I was always so timid and safe, but that was because of David. I had a child to care for, of course I wouldn't run toward danger. Anger welled in me as I thought about my late husband and the danger that I was too scared to run from. "I'd love to destroy a monster."

The town elders rose to their feet and bowed slightly. "Be careful, Mae. This beast is not of mortal origin. It's said to have been born from chaos. A remnant of a time when monsters roamed more freely. A time before heroes. When the Mythics were bored. That's when humanity is most troubled."

"I understand," I said. "I've faced my share of monsters, but to be clear, I'm no hero."

He studied me for a moment, as if trying to decide whether I could truly handle the task. After a moment, he sighed and gestured to one of the guards nearby. "Please take her to the last villager to see the monster so that she can get a heading and begin her search."

I followed the guard and spoke to a farmer who looked like he had seen a ghost.

"The monster trampled a large portion of my field and knocked in a bit of one of the walls of my house. I saw it leaving after the attack. It was headed to the northeast. Toward the Taygesian Wilds. Please help us," the man said. I couldn't shake the feeling that what he was feeling right now was a feeling that I'd been familiar with in my time on Earth. It wasn't just fear. It was fear mixed with a hopelessness that only comes with feeling completely powerless to change your situation. I hated that look, because I'd seen it almost every time I looked into a mirror during my life with Felix. I accidentally smiled at a new thought I had. I wasn't powerless anymore, in fact, I was so powerful that even the Mythic beings of this place might fear me.

"This monster will regret attacking the sanctity of your home," I said with resolve. The man nodded and gave a smile back that still felt closer to sadness somehow. When I accepted the quest. I saw another bit of text appear in my vision.

New Quest: Defeat the monster for Thermos.

I focused on my current quest and set off, my mind clear and my steps steady. The old world and its creatures held no fear for me anymore. Not when a large lion can chomp down on me and do no damage. Not when a sharp cutting tool can't even break my skin. I was trusting my invincibility more and more. This monster was going to be destroyed even if I just had to let it attack me until it was too tired to win the fight. I could play the long game.

I headed out of the city's gates around midday and opened my map to ensure that I was headed towards the Taygesian Wilds as the man suggested. I wasn't sure how long it would take me to find the monster, but I was excited at the thought of destroying it. I wasn't even worried about having to camp out for the night if I didn't find it before dark. I was really enjoying the complete lack of fear.

Chapter 7

THE SPLASH

As I walked through the trees, I enjoyed the sounds of birds and other wildlife in the surrounding forest. I was so engrossed in the soundscape that it was easy to tell when the animals became more sparse. I'd been walking for a couple of hours at least when I came up to a small river where the trees were far enough apart that I could see the sky. I guessed that it was about mid-afternoon, but it was difficult to tell with such tall trees around me. This part of the forest looked more ancient than the rest. These are woods that I would've never wandered into in the past. It reminded me of the evil looking forest in Snow White, when she runs from the huntsman and everything startles her. I wasn't scared though. That huntsman would've been scared of me.

The complete lack of animal sounds in this part of the forest was eerie. My pace had slowed and it was beginning to be too dark to travel. I found a nook in some twisted roots and laid down. A familiar owl flew down and perched nearby.

"This seems like an odd place to rest, but I guess anywhere is safe when you're invincible," said Noctua. She tilted her head and then spun it around a bit further than looked natural.

"I was more concerned about comfort than safety," I said, patting the root as if I was fluffing a pillow. I tore off a nearby chunk of moss and placed it under where my head would be.

"I'm prepared to answer a few more questions," said the wise and beautiful owl.

I took a moment to think about which question I wanted to ask first. One seemed to be the most pressing. "Am I going to have nightmares about my husband every time I sleep?"

"You'll see what you need to see. I can assure you that everything here is for a purpose. Nothing happens at random, but everything for a reason and by necessity," she answered.

"Can you tell me more about the monster I'm looking for?" I said, with more excitement than a normal person would have.

"The beginning of all wisdom is wonder," Noctua said. Then her head tilted and she added. "I have a feeling you will soon find out all you need to know."

I wasn't very happy with the lack of a good answer, but I guessed that she wasn't able to tell me or didn't know.

"Could you explain the notifications I keep seeing and some of these other elements that I don't quite understand, like what it said my class was?" I asked.

"I will explain as much as I can currently and then I will depart for now. You will get experience for killing monsters and completing quests. You'll receive notifications that are helpful in understanding how your actions are assisting in your growth. Your class is Kolossos. This class specializes in physical combat using strength and momentum. When I leave, you should think about your status menu and you'll be able to learn more. This discussion has given you plenty to digest. I will see you again in the near future." With that, she flew off. A single owl noise could be heard in the distance as she faded into the night.

"She is just the life of the party, isn't she?" I asked no one. I had gotten used to saying little sassy things to myself. Being alone didn't bother me. Not anymore.

I thought about my status menu and a new screen displayed in my vision. I assume time stopped, but I had nothing to base that theory off of. A thought occurred to me, I could easily test my theory. I thought the menu away and tossed a nearby rock in the air somewhat near the side of my vision and brought the status menu back up. I could see the rock right beside the menu. Time froze during this menu as well. I started reading the information.

Mae June Cohen

Level 1 - Kolossos

HP - 100/100

EP - 200/240

---

5 Sanguin: This humor has a direct correlation to constitution and HP.

5 Coleric: This humor has a direct correlation to speed and agility.

5 Flegmat: This humor has a direct correlation to intellect and luck.

19 Melanc: This humor has a direct correlation to strength and EP.

I focused on my class to see if I could get more information. Noctua seemed to imply that I'd get some answers from this menu. A small window popped up superimposed over the rest of the text. It startled me and when I stopped focusing on my class it disappeared. I brought it back up and actually read it this time.

> Kolossos
>
> This is a strength and momentum based class and can only be attained if the Coleric and/or Melanc humors are elevated. The amount of force that this class can produce is legendary and it grows as either of those humors grow in power. This class automatically obtains the Mighty Leap skill and the Raging Bull skill.

My eyes unfocused on the menus and refocused on the treetops above me. The Mighty Leap skill made sense of the ridiculous increase in my jumping ability, but what was the Raging Bull skill? I had an idea and could easily test it. I thought about a skills menu and one appeared. I could focus on the listed skill and get a description just like I did with my class.

There were many skills listed that seemed to cover things that one might find themselves doing on a regular basis like Athletics, Acrobatics, and Archery.

Most of them were highlighted a pinkish-red color and said 'Apraxos' next to them. As I scrolled down the list, I found Mighty Leap and then Raging Bull. These were highlighted orange and said 'Metrios' next to them. I wasn't sure what Apraxos and Metrios meant, but I could always ask about that later. If Noctua only answered a couple of questions at a time, it would take awhile to get through them.

I was hoping that I'd get a better understanding of what my new body was actually doing by reading through the skills. It was incredible to be able to harness this much power and direct it through a body that not too long ago hurt whenever I moved. The more I thought about it, the more excited I became about becoming even more powerful. I also wondered what other special skills and abilities I might be able to learn here. I refocused and read the descriptions before my mind wondered too much.

Mighty Leap (Metrios)

Squatting down for more than three seconds activates this skill. The force and angle of the leap can be decided before take off. This skill will scale with the Coleric and Melanc Humors and Acrobatics.

Raging Bull (Metrios)

Sprinting for more than three seconds activates this skill. Upon activation, this skill provides a damage bonus based on momentum at the time of collision with another object. This skill will scale with the Coleric and Melanc Humors and Athletics.

I closed my menus again. This was so different from what my life was only a few days ago. If I tried to run or jump like the skills suggested, I'd definitely have broken something. More likely, broken many some-things. I felt like a little kid trying to fall asleep before Christmas morning. I was so excited to try these skills out more in the morning. I'd get up now, but it was so dark, I doubted I could even run for three seconds without tripping. A wave of sadness washed over me as I really processed what I had just felt. I was excited to wake up the next morning. I hadn't felt that way in a long time. I closed my eyes, tried to banish that thought, and waited for sleep to take me.

My body shot up in my bed, but it wasn't my current body. I was much smaller. A loud coughing fit echoed through the basic room I now stood in. I recognized it, but I didn't want to. This was my childhood bedroom. Memories flooded back and I wanted to wake up. I couldn't. I couldn't even choose what happened in the vision, or whatever this was. It was like I was watching a movie from the perspective of a young girl. It was me and I knew it was me. The coughing continued. It sounded horrible and was probably what had woken me up in the first place.

I walked to the other small bedroom in the house where my parents slept. My mother was the one coughing. She saw me there and put one hand up in a 'stop' motion while finishing her coughing fit.

"Don't come in here, Mae. I don't want you around us when we're sick like this," she said weakly, coughing again. "Your aunt will be here in the morning to pick you up. You're going to go live with her for a bit until we're back on our feet. Back to bed with you, dear."

I couldn't focus on her words. I was too busy looking at my father's face. His head was turned toward me. He was the closest to me and their door on their bed. The blanket was down his chest far enough for me to notice that his night-shirted chest was not rising and falling. My mother must've noticed between coughing fits that I was still looking at father. She nudged him and when she realized that the nudges were becoming more frantic her motherly instinct to protect me kicked in.

"Go to your room and don't come out until your aunt gets here," she said. Tears were now streaming down her face and mine. I wanted to run to him, but I listened and retreated to my bedroom. I'll never forget the sound of my mother crying over my father's body. I had to cover my head and push my blanket against my ears to stop the noise. I didn't sleep that night.

The nightmarish vision skipped ahead to a conversation with my aunt maybe a month later. I remember it as one of the worst conversations of my life. She told me that my mother had also passed away and that I'd be living with her now. I was twelve when my parents died. My aunt did her best, but I was mostly left alone to fend for myself. The silver lining of having to go live with my aunt was her library. Her husband had been a professor of classical studies at the nearby college. All of his books were there. I remember the first book I ever pulled from his shelf. The Odyssey. It took Odysseus ten years to return home, but I knew that wasn't an option for me. Maybe that's why I was hooked.

My eyes opened and I was once again looking toward the tree tops. My eyes narrowed. Instead of being sad or angry about my childhood circumstances, I chose to focus on my circumstances right now. I was about to find a monster and defeat it. I was going to live out the adventure of the ancient Greek heroes that I'd read about all my life. Nothing was going to keep me from enjoying this. I put all of those negative feelings in a mental suitcase to unpack on a later date. I got up from my makeshift bed, feeling the power of my new body.

I squatted down for the prerequisite three seconds with a mind to use my Mighty Leap to go even deeper into this forest. Hopefully, I'd make enough of a ruckus to lure the monster over. I could see a smaller, unnamed body of water just north of me and I aimed in that direction. I put all of my strength into the jump and released. I didn't hit any large branches on the way through the canopy and I was able to see the small lake at the apex of my jump. It was maybe a fifth of the size of Lake Narcis, but I was headed directly for it. I decided to make the most of the situation.

Since I wouldn't be feeling any pain from the splashdown, I spread my body out as much as possible. The resulting splash must've been huge. I wish I could've seen it from the outside. I swam to the lake's edge which was made more difficult by my laughing. I kept laughing as I sprawled out on the ground facing the bright morning sky. I felt the coolness of shade on my face. My eyes were still closed as I enjoyed the moment. The events of the previous night and feelings they might've dredged up had fled back to the past.

I heard a snort and felt heat on my face. My eyes opened and I was face to face with the snake-eyed bullish monstrosity. It snorted again and I felt the serpentine tail wrap around my legs and lift me off of the ground. The ophiotaurus lifted my body up to meet its eyes again. I was hanging upside down in front of the monster. It was massive. I looked past its face and saw the bottom half of the trees were soaked. I couldn't help it and laughed again. That was a massive splash.

"Sorry, I'm not laughing at you. I just cannot believe that splash," I said. Before I could process the ridiculousness of apologizing to the monster, it whipped its tail around with me still ensnared in it. I went flying into a nearby tree and hit it with a sickening thud. I tumbled to the base of the tree and laughed again. This time because I didn't know how else to react. The bull-snake hybrid came slithering toward me. I was able to push off enough to dodge the first attack, but not fast enough to dodge his tail whipping at me as he stopped himself from ramming the tree. I flew again, but this time landed in a fairly large field that was relatively flat. This was the perfect opportunity to test my other Kolossos skill.

I was far enough away to get a good running start after having rolled quite a bit after landing. I began running at the monster, which must've been a strange twist for him to be the one being charged. I felt the skill engage after the initial three seconds and yelled out when I was about halfway to the monster. It was just for fun and not required in any way. "Raging Bull!"

I collided with the ophiotaurus and he recoiled back over his own tail. I took a few steps back and watched him right himself. He was obviously dazed for a moment, but quickly rose to his normal height again. I just stood there smiling. His full body rotated and he did a similar tail whip attack as before. This one was much more powerful and once again I went flying to the other side of the clearing.

"You already tried that," I yelled over to him when I stood up. We were on opposite sides of the clearing at this point and I had an idea of how to defeat him. I didn't know how many health points he had left, but this attack should do a good amount of damage. I put my pointer fingers up to either side of my head as mock bull horns. Then, I did the thing with my leg that I'd seen bulls do before they charge, like they were winding up. We ran toward each other at full speed.

He was faster than me so we met with him covering about two-thirds of the distance. There was a loud crack as his lowered head met mine. He once again snapped backward over his tail and was dazed. I was driven backwards and fell to the ground with the recoil, but I quickly righted myself and squatted down. After three seconds, I leapt into the air as high as I'd ever gone. It was mostly straight up and slightly forward. As I began to descend, I found myself fists first. I figured this plan would work whether it was feet or fists first. My aim was perfect and I ended up crashing down with both fists hitting the top of the Ophiotaurus' head. I noticed some notifications, but I ignored them for now.

He crumpled to the ground and I tumbled off to the side. I smiled. The feeling of power was better than any other feeling I could remember. I instantly knew that I wanted to face more monsters.

A large gold coin appeared above the non-moving form of the monster. He had been defeated and I had gotten a level up notification along with the quest notification.

Quest Completed: Defeat the monster for Thermos.

Chapter 8

A Reward

I went for the large gold coin first. It was suspended above the deceased monster. I grabbed it and turned it around in my hand. The coin had an image of the half bull, half snake monster on one side and the words 'one mina' on the back. I thought about storing it and it disappeared. The notification with my current coins popped into view the one mina now joined the one drachma that I had earned from moving logs. I had no idea what the difference in value was, but I could ask when I got back to Thermos. I wasn't too worried about money here as I wouldn't be spending money on swords or armor and food also didn't seem all that important.

Would the elders believe me if I just told them that I'd defeated the monster? I probably would want proof if I was them. Especially since they didn't really know me all that much. I grabbed the tail of the ophiotaurus and gave it a tug to see if I could move it. I wasn't sure if I needed to bring it back to the town leaders or not, but didn't want to have to trek all the way back. It was heavy, but I could move it. It would take a week to get it back to Thermos at this rate. I was thinking about maybe putting together a simple sled or something like that to help drag the body back, but then I remembered the other notification that had appeared when I defeated the monster. I had gained a level.

I pulled up my status menu and noted the changes. Besides being level two now, I'd automatically gained a little extra max HP and EP. Since I hadn't applied any humor points I figured that must be a benefit of leveling up. I applied all five humor points to Melanc for increased strength hoping that it would make dragging the monster body easier. I did want to increase my speed at some point, but now wasn't the time. I needed to be stronger.

Mae June Cohen
Level 2 - Kolossos
HP - 110/110
EP - 110/300

5 Sanguin: This humor has a direct correlation to constitution and HP.

5 Coleric: This humor has a direct correlation to speed and agility.

5 Flegmat: This humor has a direct correlation to intellect and luck.

24 Melanc: This humor has a direct correlation to strength and EP.

I'd have to figure out exactly what the Energy Points meant since I now had only about a third of my now larger pool left. What would happen if I ran out? I didn't think I would die or anything, but would I just fall asleep? I had no idea, but it probably wouldn't be helpful.

I was back out of menus and once again grabbed the monster's tail. It seemed slightly less imposing than it had been before, but I figured that I had just grown again when I applied the points in Melanc. When I pulled, the body moved with relative ease. I could probably get this back to town before nightfall. I headed back to Thermos with a smile on my face. It was difficult to understand exactly where the joy was coming from. The fight was fun and all, but why couldn't I stop smiling? After walking and thinking for a while, it hit me. This was the opposite of how I'd handled treacherous situations during my life. I wanted more. Not only more power though. I wanted more of this feeling.

I made good time. The sun was setting when I approached the same gate that I'd come to just a couple days ago. The same guard was on duty and I thought he was going to tumble out of his outpost and over the fence trying to see what I was dragging. Or maybe just trying to believe what I was dragging.

"Is that what I think it is?" Asked the guard. He quickly realized that he should be opening the gate and not just gawking. He ran down and opened it wide enough for me to bring my quarry in.

"It sure is!" I said, pausing to revel in my victory. "Did you doubt me?" I smiled as cutely as I could even though I was hulking over the man and dragging a dead monster.

"It's a mistake that I won't make again. You can be sure!" The guard said as he rubbed the back of his head with a hint of embarrassment. He waved me through. "I'm sure the town elders will be excited to join you in your success. They were very worried about more attacks from that beast."

I nodded at him and continued toward the center of town dragging the ophiotaurus behind me. It ended up being the perfect time to strut through town as dozens of townsfolk cheered as I passed. I reached the bench where the elders sat and flopped the tail down in front of them with a flourish.

"I finished that little quest you gave me," I said with a wink. They sat there without speaking for a while until finally one of them cleared their throat loudly and spoke up.

"This is very good news! Thank you for taking care of this monster for us, young lady. You've done the town a great service and we will reward you in our traditional way," the central elder said as the others nodded in agreement. He waved over a teenage boy and whispered something in his ear. The boy ran off as quickly as he had come.

"What's the traditional way? Like a reward? I already got this from the monster" I popped the coin with the monster's image on it into my hand and showed the elders. They seemed surprised at the coin and glanced at each other as if they were communicating telepathically or just knew what the others were thinking.

"May I see that coin?" Asked the elder who wore glasses and had been reading until now. I handed him the coin. He looked it over and turned it in his hand. "I haven't seen a coin like this for a long time and never one with this image on it. Did this appear when you defeated the ophiotaurus?"

"Yes. It was suspended above his body," I answered.

"Hmm. You could make a good living going from town to town and dealing with any monsters that they have quests out for. This coin alone is worth a hundred drachma," he said, handing the coin back to me. This was helpful information. I'd just made the equivalent to a hundred days of labor just from defeating one monster. I popped the coin away and it joined my single drachma. Another of the elders spoke next, he must've realized that my coin distraction meant I hadn't gotten an answer to my other questions.

"The traditional way of rewarding an adventurer who helps the town is through suzonumi. The whole town is being notified of what you've accomplished and how you helped Thermos and the young man we sent off is both informing and collecting. He will return shortly," said the man who was sitting to the left of the central elder.

"Well, I guess while we're waiting, could I ask you a few more questions?" I asked, smiling at the elders. I was very excited to know that I'd be getting more rewards. The young man came back after about another twenty minutes with an overloaded leather bag that used ropes instead of straps, but otherwise looked like a standard flapped backpack. The elders had explained the different denominations of coins, given a short history of this land, and had just begun talking about the Mythics.

The backpack was now sitting in front of me and the young man was down on one knee, obviously winded. He looked at me expectantly. An elder spoke up to mitigate any awkwardness.

"It is customary for the receiver of the suzonumi to provide the aggelos, in this case young Linus here, a gift for his work," said the same elder who had done a lot of the explaining.

"Linus, thank you for gathering all of this for me. I'm new here so I don't really know what is customary as a gift." I looked down into the large leather bag and saw everything from cloth to weapons. I suspected there was also some coinage in the bottom of the bag based on the sound it made when he sat it down. "Would you like some money or a sword or something else?"

Linus looked at me wide eyed and spoke with hesitation and a stutter in his voice, as if he was frightened to answer me. "My father is the owner of the farm that was partially destroyed by the beast. He has lived in constant fear of being attacked again since the initial destruction of one of our fields. He offered my grandfather's sword and many drachma to repay your kindness. He believes that you saved our family's heritage with your mighty deed." He continued to kneel, but refused to make eye contact while he spoke. It looked like he may cry.

I reached to the bottom of the bag and was able to pull the coins into my personal money stores that I still didn't quite understand. There was almost another hundred drachma all together and that didn't even count the value of the rest of the contents. This was an amazing reward. There was only one short sword in the bag so I pulled it out and held it in front of the young man.

"Take your grandfather's sword and keep it in your family," I said, offering him the sword. He took the sword, bowed low, and thanked me with tears beginning to run down his face. Then, he ran off. I'd guessed that he was running back home to tell his father the good news. I felt pretty good about myself. Is this what heroes feel like all the time? As he continued to run into the distance, the mom in me flared up and I wanted to yell at him to stop running with a sharp object, but I stopped myself. This wasn't my world.

"That was unexpected," said the central elder. "I've never seen a champion give that big of a gift to their aggelos and certainly never a weapon of that quality. That sword could've been sold for close to fifty drachma. They may still sell it to rebuild their farm, but you've given them hope."

I thanked the elders and slung the bag over one arm. I had something else that I wanted to do before I left to find another town. I liked the hunting down quests and monsters idea. I'd be able to see more of this beautiful land and I always wanted to travel when I was on Earth. This was my chance. I waved as I walked in the same direction that Linus had ran off. I didn't really need money for gear with my new body and abilities. I was going to do one more heroic thing before I left.

As I walked, I began to think about why I was so driven to help this young man and his family. After about five minutes, I had it pretty much figured out. My late husband had sold almost everything of value that we had owned by the end of his life. This had included every thing that still remained from my parents. I didn't have much, but my prized possessions had been my father's watch and mother's locket. I was pretty sure that these were the only things of value that they had when they passed and I had gotten them.

He had sold them without telling me under the guise of helping our family. I knew it was more the fact that he had once again wasted our monthly stipend from Uncle Sam to fuel his habits. The anger washed over me, but so did the resolve to not let this young man lose his grandfather's sword or their family farm because of the destructive power of an uncontrolled monster.

I found the partially destroyed farm and a middle-aged man working in a nearby barn. "Are you Linus' father?" I asked. He turned and saw me approaching and sat his pitchfork down.

"Yes, I'm his father. My name is Rovertos," the man said. A look of worry flashed across his face. "Did he do something wrong? Is this about my father's sword? Was he not supposed to bring it back to me? Please, take it, Champion. We meant no disrespect." The man lowered himself to his knees and looked up at me almost looking like he would start crying as well. It was obvious that he hadn't been sleeping much and the worry lines were pronounced on his face.

"Whoa, whoa. Nothing like that. Your son didn't do anything wrong. He did leave before I could finish giving him the gift for his work in gathering the suzonumi for me though," I said as quickly as possible to stop the man from falling further into his panic.

"What? You already gave him my father's sword back. That is an exorbitant gift. I first thought that either he'd made up the story, or stolen it back somehow," said the man. I extended my hand and helped him to his feet. He stood about a foot shorter than me, but had the strong build of a lifetime farmer.

"Please, call me Mae. If you'd indulge me, what was the cost of your lost crops and the cost to rebuild the wall of your home?" I asked. The man was taken aback by my question, but I could see the relief that his son wasn't in trouble.

"Well, Mae, I'm glad to hear that he didn't wrong you in some way. It would've been foolish to do something like that to someone who could defeat an ophiotaurus," he said with a smile and then thought for a moment. He must've been figuring costs in his head. "The field was not fully destroyed and I was able to save much of the crop. The house will be our main expense. Probably almost forty drachma in total, but that's less than the worth of my father's sword. I didn't know how we'd pay for everything, but you've provided a way." There was a twinge of sadness, even though overall I could tell he was glad that he had a way to provide for his family still.

"Would you do just one other thing for me for defeating the beast and giving you back your father's sword?" I asked.

"Anything, Mae. My family is in your debt," he said.

"Take this and use it to rebuild and cover your losses. I'd like for you to not have to sell your father's sword," I said, holding out my hand and producing ten silver coins. These silver coins were worth four drachma each. The only way I knew this was that I'd thought about taking out forty drachma and these coins appeared. His faced went from confused to almost shaking his head in the negative. I thought he was about to refuse my offer.

"I won't take no for an answer." I quickly added, raising an eyebrow. He went rigid at the seriousness of my tone, but I wasn't trying to threaten him. I dissolved the tension with an added, "please."

Now, he was full on crying. "As you wish, Mae. I vow that this sword will stay in my family for as long as I can promise it. Thank you for your kindness. My family will forever look to you as a hero and the story of your victory and generosity will be passed down with the sword." He bowed and went back to his work after wiping his face. His anxiety had completely melted away. This was what I was here for. I

couldn't wait to visit the next town and fight my next
monster.

Chapter 9

The Beach

By the time I'd finished up with the farmer, it was well into the evening and I wanted to sleep. The sleep was more just to get me to the next morning than it was a necessity, although I did need my energy topped off and sleep would accomplish that. I headed back to the Golden Hearth and my room was still available. I gave Xenia a drachma in exchange for meals and my room for the night. The stew she had over the fire was great and I went to bed ready to head out the next morning.

I woke up from a fairly undisturbed sleep. The only interruption came in the form of a brief look back to a Christmas early in my marriage. Felix sat in his recliner with his thousand yard stare while our toddler David opened one of the small presents I had scrounged up and wrapped for him. We didn't have a tree or any decorations that year. The juxtaposition of the joy my son found and whatever it was that his father was experiencing was disturbing. My late husband had ruined many holidays, but I made sure that David always had some sort of joy.

The excitement of heading to the next town made it easy to shove anything that I saw in my sleep away. I wasn't going to let that man ruin my time here as well. I exited my room to find Xenia at her counter.

"Did you sleep well, dear?" The sweet woman asked.

"Well enough," I said, pulling up a stool and taking a seat. "I'm going to head out soon. Do you have any suggestions for what town I should head to next?"

"If I could travel anywhere, I'd probably head to Cythara to the south. It is a beautiful town on an island in the Naxion Sea," she answered.

"That sounds good to me. Don't worry though, I'm sure that I'll be back at some point," I said, as she brought me a couple of well cooked eggs. I ate them quickly and stood to leave. "Thanks for everything, Xenia."

She came around the counter to give me a hug. The height difference was fairly humorous at this point as she stood about a foot and a half shorter than me. I wondered how much larger I'd be the next time around. I was excited to level up and to keep getting stronger.

I left through the south gate and opened my map. I estimated a few hours of travel would get me to the coast, then I'd have to find a boat. I wasn't sure exactly how fast the boats moved here, but I figured on maybe a week at most to reach the island of Cythara. I was grateful to have a built in map and that Melosia, the first town I'd visited, had a world map to fill in many of the details of this land. I tried out the strongest Mighty Leap that I could muster and noted on my map where I was before the jump. This is how I learned that I could mentally pin locations and even scribble in little notes. I pinned the start of my jump.

When I landed, I was almost halfway to the coast. My strength had really improved. I'd have to do more testing to see what I could really do. That last monster must've weighed over a ton. At first, it was a struggle, but after I had applied my points and my strength had grown, I could drag it fairly easily. I decided on the simple test of punch a nearby tree. The haymaker connected with a thud that would've ensured many broken bones in my hand and arm if not for my invincibility. I did leave a mark, but it didn't explode into splinters or anything.

I decided to run the last half for two reasons. The first was that I didn't want to accidentally jump directly into the large body of water. The second was that I didn't exactly know what to expect. My map had filled in the bigger cities and landmarks, but there had to be more small settlements or villages around. I wasn't one hundred percent sure about that, but it seemed like solid logic. Another added bonus was the joy I felt in using my new body. I found myself smiling as I thought about my new capabilities versus my old frail body. I was beginning to feel so alive, which was ironic because of the whole dying experience.

The last half of the journey was quiet. I had plenty of time to enjoy my beautiful surroundings, but I had secretly hoped for another surprise monster or something. I came to a clearing at the edge of the forest and saw that there were hilly plains between myself and the ocean. Now that I could see further, I tried one more Mighty Leap and landed close enough to smell the salty water.

I heard the gulls beckoning me to the sea. As I crested the last ridge, I was encouraged to see a couple of ships in the waters just off the coastline. I looked up and down the coast and saw a port town to the southwest. It wasn't on the map that I had, so I figured that the seven cities that were on it were probably just the larger ones. This port town was definitely smaller than Thermos and much more so than Melosia. I'd made my way toward this new town with a lovely stroll down the beach. It wasn't a well maintained beach which is to say it wasn't what you'd find at a resort. There were logs and washed up bits of board.

I realized as I walked past that the boards were chunks of ship hulls. I could clearly make out a large, broken off rib of a ship with splintered boards attached. The logs turned out to be destroyed ship masts. This section of beach must've been where the current and waves naturally deposited both the flotsam and the jetsam. I continued toward the town thinking this was all perfectly logical thinking. It wasn't until I got closer to the town that I began to question my assumptions.

A young girl, maybe in her mid-teens, shouted at me from the edge of the beach that the town abutted. "Get off the beach! Quickly!" She frantically waved me over. Her head darted from me to the ocean as I walked along without a care in the world. I jogged over the last bit as she became more exasperated.

"What's wrong? Why do you seem so excited, young one?" I asked. The tone was supposed to be in my comforting, sweet grandma voice, but she didn't seem comforted. In fact, she looked exceedingly confused.

"Did you not notice the wreckage?" She asked.

"Oh, I noticed the bits of wood. Nothing to be this excited about though," I said, gesturing back toward the beach. She looked at me like I was juggling cats. It was a mixture of fear and bewilderment.

"Didn't you wonder what happened to the ship?" She asked. It was the way a teen asks something that makes you feel stupid, but you're not sure why. Before I could answer, I saw a look of fear splash across her face and then she turned and ran away. I turned to see what had caused the strange reaction.

The water bulged up as if Godzilla was rising from the depths, but this was wider than what I'd seen in those old movies. As the surface tension broke, I saw a couple of crab eyes poking out of the water. They appeared to be scanning the beach. I didn't think that it had seen me yet, but it was difficult to tell. It rose up even more from the water and I confirmed it to be a giant crab. I estimated it to be about as wide as a school bus is long, maybe forty feet or so and about thirty feet from front to back.

The monster crustacean's claws came up next as it moved closer to the beach. Each claw was the size of a VW bug. The last part to come ashore was the monster's legs, but they weren't legs at all. Tentacles protruded from the bottom half of the crab. This was some kind of crab and octopus hybrid monster. It picked up the longest piece of a ship's mast that was angled in its way and snipped it in two with a claw like it was a toothpick. The cut was at an angle and the two halves were about eight to ten feet in length. This thing could do a lot of damage.

It's mandibles were moving around like it was eating something, but I couldn't see anything in it's mouth. It pushed aside a few chunks of wood and I realized something. It wasn't eating, it was tasting the air. It was following the same line that I'd walked down the beach. Could it smell me? It stopped in it's tracks and its body rose up a bit. I think it spotted me. The crabtopus was about half a football field away and began moving more quickly in my direction. This also happened to be in the direction of the little port town, so I decided to help it change direction.

I squatted down and waited. It had covered about half of the distance by the time I leapt into the air. It snapped its claws at me, but it was too slow and I was still slightly out of range. I landed behind it and got its attention again.

"Hey! Over here crabby-pus!" I yelled. It shifted and began to turn toward me. It wasn't very quick on land, especially when attempting a hundred eighty degree turn. The octopus type tentacles were no doubt better in the water. Water. A terrible thought that I hadn't considered crossed my mind. Could I drown? I was invincible to physical damage sure, but did I still have to breath. I started to have a small panic attack where I was hyper focused on my breathing, but I couldn't tell if I was breathing. I tried to take in a deep breath, but I was too panicked to remember how.

The creature grabbed me with a tentacle and slammed me into the sand. I still couldn't tell if I was breathing and this new development certainly wasn't helping. I got slammed over and over again, creating a deeper and deeper crater in the soft sand. It released me and I scrambled to my feet, unharmed. I threw a chunk of wood at the monster which flew toward one of its eyestalks. The eyestalk retracted at the last second and then popped back into place. The wood glinted harmlessly off of the crab monster's hard shell and fell back to the beach.

I didn't know how to tell if a crab was mad, but it seemed mad as it took me into one of its massive claws. I could feel pressure as it attempted to snip me in half like it had with the thick log of wood that was the piece of ship's mast. No matter how hard it tried, I just refused to separate. It began shaking its claw and seemed to be getting exasperated. I used one of the moments of looser grip to wedge my feet up and into the claw. I used all of my strength and pushed out with my powerful legs. The claw began to open, but this was met with more pressure.

I was in the squatted position at this point and it gave me an idea. I attempted to activate my Mighty Leap skill and to my surprise, it worked. The skill-assisted force bent the smaller part of the claw back with a sickening snap. The crabtopus let out a weird hiss, that must've been the crab equivalent to 'ouch'. I fell down to the sand and stood up again.

"That's what you get for being rude to a total stranger and to that boat. I'm assuming that was you," I said. I knew it was nonsense to speak to a giant crab and octopus monster, but this whole scenario was a little nonsensical. It slid over and tried to use its other claw to snip me in half, but after a few minutes of trying and failing, it just tossed me into the sand again.

I needed to figure out how to defeat this thing. An arial attack was probably out of the question as any shelled area was essentially thick armor. The answer had to be in its underbelly, where the tentacles sprouted from. That had to be a weak point. I scanned the beach, desperately trying to formulate a method to kill this thing before it tried to drag me under the water and drown me. I spotted the two halves of mast that the monster had snipped in half when it first emerged. They were quite sharp from the diagonal cut.

I didn't want to lose my nice backpack that had somehow remained intact this whole time so I removed it during this brief pause in the fighting. Maybe the monster was trying to figure out how to kill me as well. As I sat the bag down in the crater that my body had created, I remembered that there had been a dagger in it. There was something that I kind of wanted to try since I saw it in an old pirate movie, but it seemed too dangerous to be practical. I had no worries of cutting my mouth now though.

I ran over to the sharp logs and picked one up as a test. I had both my hands available as the dagger was clamped securely in my teeth the whole time. I wanted a way to defend myself if it grabbed me with its tentacles. The log was much lighter than I remembered the others being, but I'd also grown in strength. Throwing it like a javelin was out of the question as it was just too thick around for that. The idea hit me like a piece of wood which had been flung by a giant crab. It had another weakness in its inability to turn quickly.

As it rotated to locate another projectile, I saw how much difficulty it had on land. It also didn't seem to have great vision. I would use these weaknesses to my advantage. I used both hands to jab the first log, pointy side up, into the sand. I dodged another thrown piece of ship and planted the other piece about five feet away from the first. I was able to bury them about two to three feet deep and they felt sturdy. I'd leave them there and go to the next phase. I was really hoping that this monster had the crab brain and not the much more intelligent octopus brain.

I took the dagger out of my mouth and ran toward the monster. There was plenty of room between the tentacles and I was able to run underneath it and slice at the soft, unarmored tentacles. This plan wouldn't have worked at all if this thing had had regular crab legs. It made the strange hissing noises as it tried to grab me while I cut at it. I knew that I wasn't going to be taking it out this way, but I figured that I could at least make it a little angry at me.

When it was turned away from the sharp logs, I sprinted toward them. It turned and found its target and began shifting toward me. I ran far enough past the posts that they were out of range to be used as weapons. That's what I'd hoped it would think anyway. I had to time this right for it to have any hope of working. The monster started crawling toward me as I had hoped.

When the monster was positioned right over the secured mast pieces, I leapt into the air. If I could see my desired landing zone, I found that I could have confidence in the accuracy of the strike. I knew the armor would protect the top, but I was just trying to transfer energy downward. My hope was that the cuts I put into the tentacles would weaken them enough to let the monster drop to the ground when I jumped onto its back.

The timing and aim worked out perfectly. I landed near the middle of the monster's back. It forcefully dropped to the sand with the downward force of my landing and let out a terrible hiss as the twin impalement spikes slid into its soft underbelly. It wasn't defeated though. Its claws came to find me on its back, but I was able to duck and they snapped above my head. As I squatted down for a moment, I had another idea. I leapt straight up which once again provided the necessary downward force for another set of stabs.

I landed hard on the monster's sturdy carapace and this final downward force was enough to finish off the mighty beast. The floating gold coin appeared and I took it into my personal funds. I heard clapping and cheers. Looking around, I poked my confused head over the top of the monster and saw a line of villagers along with that same young girl that I'd first seen. She must've gone and brought friends to the show.

"That was amazing!" One of them yelled over to me.

"We can finally use this beach again," yelled another. Another round of cheers rose up.

I laid back on the hard shell of the monster and rested for a bit. I closed my eyes and smiled. Although, I still didn't know if I could drown here. I'd leave that worry for another day. I loved beating up monsters and I knew that this was only the beginning.

Chapter 10

HERE FOR

I hopped down and grabbed my leather backpack. I decided to just toss the knife into the bag as I didn't have a good way of attaching it to my waist at the moment. I turned back to the group that had come from the town and they were already at the body of the crab monster poking and prodding it.

"What are we going to do with the body and the wreckage?" I asked one of the adults that was present.

"We'll have to get the mayor involved for questions like that," said the man as he gestured back toward the port town. "Oh, here he comes now. I'll go tell him what happened." The man jogged over to another man who was walking toward the gathered mass of people. I saw the two of them talk briefly and then the first man I was speaking to pointed at me. The mayor came over to me and held out his hand to shake mine.

He was a portly man who looked just stately enough to be a mayor.

"I hear that some thanks are in order. That beast was really beginning to put a damper on the fishing that we rely on here in Lysandria. This was the third vessel in recent months to have been destroyed. We are in your debt and you are welcomed to Lysandria as our hero," said the man with a deep bow. "If you don't object, I'd love to throw a feast with you as the guest of honor."

"I'd love to celebrate with you and the rest of the town. I was really just passing through on my way to Cythara, but I don't have a strict timeline on when I need to get there," I said.

"Excellent! Tonight we'll all eat our fill and retell the tale of how," he paused as he realized something. "In my excitement, I'm afraid that I never asked your name."

"I'm Mae. Pleasure to meet you," I said with a courteous nod.

"Tonight we will eat our fill and retell the tale of how the mighty Mae defeated this monstrous beast!" He shouted to the crowd. This earned him a loud cheer of approval.

"What's on the menu?" I asked, figuring on some kind of seafood.

"This monstrous beast," he repeated. I wasn't wrong that it was going to be seafood, but I wasn't quite expecting this answer. He must've noticed my reaction as he quickly added, "We know how to cook here in Lysandria, I assure you that it is perfectly safe. You won't be disappointed, Mae."

"I just didn't know you could eat monster," I said, looking over at the giant, tentacled crab. The mayor smiled and put a reassuring hand on my shoulder. He had to reach up a bit.

"It will be a glorious meal," he said confidently. "My name is Mayor Perseus by the way. Feel free to explore the town a bit while I get everything prepared here on the beach. When you finish exploring the town and maybe visit some of our shops, you can meet me back here."

I nodded my agreement and walked along the beach at a relaxed pace. The rush of victory was still coursing through me and the power was something that would've helped me quite a bit during my regular life. That life and those problems were ancient history now.

As I walked to the town, I thought about the heroic Perseus that I remembered from books I had in my library. I guess this place wasn't an exact match with what I'd read, but I was fine with it. I'd just have to be open to people having names that don't necessarily match their mythology. It was still pretty awe-inspiring just to be here. Just before I arrived at the edge of Lysandria, I pulled the second large gold coin out and examined it. This one was also worth one hundred drachma according to my convenient, possibly magic coin storage. The coin had an engraved image of the crab monster on it. I glanced at it and then popped it away again as I entered the town. I was pretty sure that I'd be set on funds for a while at this rate.

The town was situated in three concentric rings with an open marketplace with stalls in the center. The inner circle was mostly shops with living spaces attached or above. There was also an inn and eatery in the inner circle. The middle was all residential as far as I could tell and the outer ring looked to be more commercial or storage. I hadn't explored it fully, but I felt that I had made a fairly accurate assessment.

I didn't care too much about anything besides the marketplace. I wanted to make sure I had whatever supplies I would need for a sea voyage and time on an island that I knew nothing about. I stopped by the blacksmith first as I had one thing that I wanted to make sure I had time to acquire. I was greeted by a gruff looking man with ash covering at least half of his face.

"Welcome to Hephaestus's Forge," he said as he refocused on the bit of metal he'd been heating when I'd entered. "I'll be with you shortly."

"Thank you, I'll just take a look at your sales counter over here, Hephaestus," I said, turning toward the display items. I noticed a smile and a slight head shake before I'd fully turned. A few minutes passed and he quenched his project and walked over to me.

"The name's Vulcon. You must be new around here. Hephaestus is one of the Mythics and he spends most of his time in Cythara. He's the Mythic who gets a cut from all of the blacksmith shops across the land. That's why this shop bears his name. Even though my family built this place and worked it for generations," he said. The last part seemed to be a sore spot as he did not seem happy with the arrangement.

"I am fairly new here, but even I know that sounds like a bad deal. My name is Mae. I just defeated the crab monster down at the beach and the mayor said there will be a party and food there tonight. He told me to come check out the shops beforehand which brought me here," I said. His eyes went wide before his demeanor changed to one that was much more cheerful.

"I know better than to miss out on free food. That's a great thing you've done. One of my best friends almost died during that last ship attack. I'll help you as best I can, Mae. I'll even give you the family discount," the man said with a slight bow.

I pulled out the dagger and showed it to the blacksmith. "I'd like to get a sheath or something for this dagger so that I can wear it around my waist for emergencies. Do you have something like that?" I asked.

"I don't usually work with too much leather, but I do trades with the leather smith for scabbards and such. My recommendation for an adventurer such as yourself, especially if you plan on taking on more monsters, is something a bit more substantial. A nice two-handed sword perhaps," he said, pointing to a large sword displayed on the wall behind him.

"I'm more of a hands and feet fighter. I just have the dagger for practicality's sake," I answered quickly before he could pull the sword down off of the wall.

"I'd still recommend a better dagger. This one is more something that you'd use on a farm, not to fight monsters. Don't you want something that will hold an edge?" He asked. I could tell by the way he spoke that he was passionate about people being properly equipped.

"Okay, well what do you recommend?" I asked. He pulled a slightly larger dagger with a unique curve to it off of the wall.

"This would be what I'd carry in your situation. It's called a kopis." He handed me the beautifully made dagger which came with a leather sheath. I gave it a few practice swings and it felt good. I put the blade to my finger to try and feel how sharp it was. This did nothing as I couldn't be cut. This made the blacksmith cringe a little as he must've thought that I'd pressed too hard. He came over to me and grabbed the finger that I'd tested against.

"I sharpen my blades with more care than any other blacksmith I've met. How is your finger unharmed?" Asked Vulcon.

"Oh, um, I didn't press it to my finger very hard," I said, trying not to raise suspicion. He raised an eyebrow in response. He went over to a small basket sitting on his workbench and pulled out a bunch of grapes. He took a grape and barely pressed it to the blade's edge. The grape instantly split with no resistance. This was all done right in front of me to illustrate his point. "Can I share something with you in confidence?"

"Of course. I take the trust of my customer's very seriously," he said, motioning me to continue.

"I have been given a gift," I said. His face went from confusion to terror and then back to confusion as I grabbed the kopis and swung it against my outstretched forearm. It just bounced off harmlessly.

"Are you a Mythic being?" He asked. He kept looking back and forth from my arm to the blade in disbelief.

"No, nothing like that. I just have the gift of invincibility. I've had it even since I got here," I said.

"You're right to keep this to yourself. The Mythics are always jockeying for the highest position of power here, although that's mostly Zeus and his two brothers. The others have pretty much etched out what they have power over when it comes to us regular folks. Hephaestus has the deal with blacksmiths, Demeter has something similar with farmers, and on and on. They all take their cut and they would hate for someone to upset the applecart," he said. He seemed pretty upset when talking about the Mythics.

"Like taxes?" I asked. Vulcon harrumphed at my question, but his irritation wasn't directed at me.

"More like insurance," he said. "They are very powerful."

I felt rage starting to rise in me at the thought of all these people living in fear. Then, I smiled as this intense anger triggered a thought.

"I think I know what I'm here for," I said. I smiled and left it at that. I made a deal with Vulcon for the kopis and found myself ten Drachma, and my previous dagger, lighter. It was a great deal, but I'd gotten something so much more valuable than a sharp blade. I left the blacksmith shop with purpose. These Mythic beings were going to find out what I was capable of. First, I needed to get stronger and I needed some questions answered. The last couple of times that I needed questions answered, Noctua showed up and helped me out. I hoped that I'd see her again soon.

I walked through the other shops that were currently open in the central ring of the town. By the time I'd finished in the blacksmith, some of the other shops had closed for the day. Based on what shops were closed, I figured that these particular people were needed to set up the big event tonight. A shop that sold fishing supplies was open, but I only bought a length of rope that could fit in my bag and moved on. The food selling shops were closed and I already had a couple changes of clothes, so I didn't buy anything in the shop called Athena's Attire. I remembered Athena being more about wisdom in ancient Greek mythology, but she was a pretty good weaver too.

I skipped the one that sold pottery and things of that sort as I had no need for anything like that. Also, I was worried that I may accidentally break something. I am quite a bit larger than most people and the shop looked fairly cramped with very breakable goods.

The last shop before completing the circle had a sign with winged shoes on it and it said 'The Talaria'. I supposed that this was the shop that Hermes got a cut of, but that was just based on the image of his iconic shoes. I walked in and this was just a general store with a little bit of everything. They did have sandals, but also goods that looked used. It was like half pawnshop and half leather goods. I was able to get some sturdy leather sandals that the shop owner assured me could handle anything I could throw at them. I questioned that confidence, but I also knew how much force any footwear would have to endure with my constant running and jumping.

I walked through the city that looked like it had been plucked straight from the pages of one of my books. I loved the stone work and the style. I must've been engrossed in taking everything in as the next thing I knew, the sun was beginning to set. I reoriented myself and headed toward the beach.

The beach was packed with people. There were at least a few hundred people sitting on the surprisingly cleared beach. All of the ship parts had been removed and the crab monster was noticeably shorter. The whole bottom half of the crab as well as its claws had been removed and could be seen cooking on a few massive nearby fires. The fires informed me of where a lot of the scrap wood had gone.

The mayor saw me from where he was directing some of the last minute set up and he waved me over. I went over to him and waited for him to finish issuing his requests.

"Looks like everything in town went well," Mayor Perseus said, pointing to my new kopis and footwear.

"Yeah, that's a pretty great town you've got there. Nice people," I said.

"Would you join me for dinner? I've got a nice central spot reserved," he said, gesturing to a large blanket with a few other people already sitting on it. "This is my wife, Andromeda, and my daughter, Georgia." I recognized his daughter as the girl in her mid-teens that I'd spoken with when I first arrived. She was the one who had tried to warn me about the monster.

"Of course," I said. Then, I whispered to him so that no one else could hear. "You won't ask me to speak in front of all these people, will you?"

"Georgia saw the whole fight and has a talent for story-telling. Would you be okay with her telling the tale?" He asked.

"That would be great. I had another request, if now is a good time?" I asked, back to a regular volume now that my nerves were calmed.

"Of course," he said.

"You did quite a service for Lysandria. What can we do in return?" Asked Andromeda.

"I just have some questions about the Mythics. Once the festivities wind down, that is," I said.

"We'd love to answer your questions," said the mayor.

"Excellent," I said with a smile. The more I knew about these Mythics, the closer I was to finding their weaknesses.

Chapter 11

THE MYTHICS

The food was great as was the retelling of the fight with the crab monster. Georgia was surprisingly good at projecting and making the story even more exciting than it really was. After the story, it was time for the part of the evening that I was most excited about though. Everyone was just relaxing on their blankets enjoying the cool evening air.

"How many Mythics are there?" I asked the mayor and his wife. Their daughter had gone off with one of her friends, so I figured it was as good a time as ever to start gathering data.

"You must be new here," said Andromeda, smiling over at her husband. It gave me a twinge of sadness thinking back to my marriage. "Twelve Mythics descended from Olympus and have residences in various cities. Zeus and Hera still live there. There could be more Mythics, I guess, but those are the ones that make themselves known to the regular people."

"Do all twelve get a cut of different businesses? Vulcon was telling me about Hephaestus getting drachma from all the blacksmiths," I said, trying not to betray my feelings about the whole situation.

"Something like that. How in depth are you wanting to go with this?" Asked the mayor.

"This is just all so different then where I come from and I thought it'd be good to know who they are, what their areas of influence are, and what the people get out of the relationship," I said. There was maybe a little more sassiness in my tone than I was intending, but they laughed it off.

"Oh, is that all," said Andromeda.

"I don't mind going through the information with you, but I'd be careful how you speak about them. Some people are under the impression that they could receive special treatment or even drachma for bringing Mythics information about nay-sayers. I've never seen one of these interactions, but you hear rumors. Usually, it doesn't seem worth it. Plus, there are people that believe the Mythics do something to bless the lands and businesses of those that support them and sometimes they are kind of radical in their response to people who talk poorly about the Mythics. I've always felt that the drachma we give the Mythics is to keep them from destroying us more than to get anything positive from them," said the mayor.

"I understand and I appreciate the words of caution. I'll be careful," I said.

"The big three are the brothers Zeus, Poseidon, and Hades. Zeus gets his tributes from town leaders which are basically just an additional tax on their towns. Poseidon gets his tributes from the fishing trade and vessel captains. Hades gets a tribute of all inheritances when a person passes away and from any drachma that changes hands on the island of Hades. Most people agree that Hades has the worst situation of the three. They are also the only three with massive stone statues. Any questions so far?" Asked Perseus.

"That all seems to match up with what I understand about those three," I said. I motioned for him to continue.

"The other Mythics are Hera, Demeter, Athena, Apollo, Artemis, Ares, Aphrodite, Hephaestus, and Hermes. Hera gets a tribute from dowries and weddings. Demeter gets a cut from farmers. Athena gets a tribute from anything having to do with education and woven items. Apollo takes his cut from medical care. Artemis gets a tribute from hunters, both when they purchase their gear and when hunters sell meat and furs. Ares gets a tribute from armies and their suppliers. Aphrodite gets a tribute from beauty related businesses and from a holiday that celebrates love. Some people think she just made up the holiday so that people would buy presents for their loved ones of which she gets a cut. Hephaestus takes from the blacksmiths and Hermes from the general and shoe stores. That's pretty much how it works out, but there is sometimes some overlap which can cause some extra stress," he said.

"Everyone has to keep their own records and complete a tribute payment every year. Most are so scared of what the Mythics could do to them or their families if they don't pay or if they mess up the accounting," added Andromeda.

"It doesn't sound like a good system to me. Why do people put up with it?" I asked.

"What choice do they have?" Asked Andromeda. "The Mythics have so much power and they have none by comparison. Zeus can throw lightning. Hades can reanimate a skeleton army. How would a normal human fight forces like that?"

"They can't, but if I get strong enough, I believe I can," I said. Based on the looks on their faces, I probably shouldn't have. They both looked around quickly to see if anyone else had heard.

"Mae, you can't say things like that. If word got back to the Mythics that you were threatening them, they'd do everything in their power to destroy you," said Andromeda.

"I'd love for the people of Lysandria and the rest of the land to not have to pay tributes, but you can't talk like that out in the open. It puts others at risk, Mae. You may be strong, but we're just regular folk. We are much more easily destroyed than you are," said the mayor. He had come closer to me and was speaking quietly.

"I'm sorry. I will be more careful," I said to both of them. "Is there a town quest board or any other monsters nearby that I could take of to build up my strength some more before I find a boat south?"

"The crab monster was our main concern. There are always sea monsters here and there, but we just try to avoid them," said Perseus.

"What about the monster that turns people to stone?" Andromeda asked her husband.

"I had almost forgotten. It's been a couple of years since anyone from our town was turned to stone and it's mostly harmless," he said.

"Mostly harmless? How is turning to stone mostly harmless?" I asked.

"They are only stone for a brief period of time, maybe a day or two, then they are back to normal. If you're interested, you should talk to Petros. He was one of the last ones to return after being turned to stone briefly," said Andromeda.

"Actually, he is probably here still," said the mayor. Then, he turned to a man nearby. "Could you put a call out for Petros to come talk to me?" The man jogged off and we returned to our blanket and conversation.

Another man jogged over a few minutes later and sat down near the mayor.

"Mae, this is Petros. Petros, could you tell Mae what you know about the monster that turned you to stone?" After the mayor's question, the man seemed to lose some of his tenseness. He must've thought he was in trouble or something.

"Absolutely. I was hunting in the forest almost straight west from town in the Elysian Wilds when I found a cave. It was right on the edge of the woods where they meet the mountains south of Olympus. I thought maybe there would be a bear or wolf in the cave, so I scouted it out. I heard a woman speak behind me. I turned and the next thing I remember, I was waking up in the middle of the forest. Based on when I got home, I figured that I must've been out for a day or so. I came back with backup about a week later. I saw the two others I had brought with me turn to stone right in front of my eyes, then it all faded again. The three of us woke up in the woods again and we spread the word for other hunters to avoid that spot," said Petros.

"Thank you. I think that was all we needed. I appreciate you taking the time to tell us what happened," said the mayor as he shook the man's hand. Petros began to walk off, but then stopped and turned back.

"If you figure out a solution, would you let me know? It'd be nice to not have to avoid the whole west side of the forest. Plus, that whole situation has always bothered me," said Petros.

"Of course. I'll let you know when it's taken care of," I said confidently. At least if I got turned to stone, I knew it wasn't permanent. At first I had thought about leaving this one alone, but I really needed to level up my strength some more.

The party dwindled down and the mayor and his wife offered me their guest room for the night. I accepted. The room was a fairly basic, second-story bedroom. There was a window, which I opened to the cool breeze and the sound of distant ocean waves.

I fell asleep with my feet hanging off the bottom of the bed, but I was content. I'd always wanted to travel to the ocean. My troubled sleep featured a memory of me begging my late husband to take us to the beach. He ended the conversation, if you could call it that, the same way he often did. First with yelling, then violence, and then an extended period of silence. I woke up startled, which was now my standard reaction to these visions of my previous life. A mixture of anger and sadness. I was startled again when I noticed the shadow in the window.

"I'm sorry, Mae. I was just here to answer questions," said Noctua. The talking owl was perched in the open window.

"I think I got most of my questions answered earlier, no thanks to you. I did have a few follow-ups though," I said, taking a deep breath and sitting up in the bed. She ignored the intended slight and looked ready to answer questions. "I think I figured out why I'm here."

"That's not a question," she said, matter-of-factly.

"I was getting to it. I'm going to stop the Mythics from taking advantage of the people here. Am I on the right track?" I asked.

"The powerful exact what they can and the weak have to comply. It is right to feel the weight of injustice in such situations," said Noctua.

"So, I'm on the right track then?" I asked.

"It is never right to do wrong or to requite wrong with wrong, or when we suffer evil to defend ourselves by doing evil in return. Think on this as you continue on your adventure," said Noctua. Then, she flew off before I could ask anymore questions.

"So, don't fight evil with evil? Two wrongs don't make a right? That's the big advice?" I asked the rhetorical questions to the empty room.

I laid back down in bed and thought about what I'd learned about the Mythics and what Noctua had said. Soon, the early morning light filled the room and I headed out for the day. Andromeda was the only person I saw on the way out of the house. She thanked me again and wished me luck on my journey.

I headed straight west out of Lysandria and was soon walking in another forest. These trees didn't look quite so ancient and spooky as the ones in the Taygesian Wilds. I felt safe as I walked through the woods. I think the fight with the giant crab who tried and failed to snip me in half gave me a lot of confidence in my invincibility gift. The only enemies I came up against between the town and the cave was a group of about a dozen large wolves. I tried clacking a couple of sticks together to scare them off, but they really wanted to fight. Punching and kicking worked just fine against the large wolves. When the fight was over, I got a notification that I was happy to receive. I had gained a level.

Mae June Cohen

Level 3 - Kolossos

HP - 120/120

EP - 293/340

5   Sanguin: This humor has a direct correlation to constitution and HP.

7   Coleric: This humor has a direct correlation to speed and agility.

5   Flegmat: This humor has a direct correlation to intellect and luck.

27   Melanc: This humor has a direct correlation to strength and EP.

Along with the level, I'd gained a small stack of drachma. I guess only the larger beasts provided a reward. It was better than carrying a bunch of pelts or monster teeth around. I could get used to this adventuring lifestyle. I thought back and realized that

I must've been close to leveling up after the fight with the giant crab monster and these wolves were just enough to push me over the edge. I had applied two points in Coleric for more speed and agility and the other three in Melanc for more strength. I had really debated just throwing them all in strength, but I wanted to test just how much of a change the points in speed would provide. I tried running and I did notice a noticeable increase in my top speed. This should also pay some dividends with my Raging Bull skill as it utilized both of those attributes. I didn't think it was enough of a benefit to do that every time, but I could cross that bridge when I get to it.

I quickened my pace toward the general area of the cave. I was able to find it pretty easily as it could be spotted from the edge of the woods. I walked over to it, checking left and right as I got closer.

"Hello?" I called into the cave. I wasn't really built for stealth, so I didn't worry about it too much. I took a tentative step in and called out again. I heard no response. I debated going in any further, as I didn't have a light source with me and caves are traditionally pretty dark. I could just wait at the edge of the woods and see if I caught a glimpse of anything.

"Wow, you're a big one," said a voice behind me. It sounded like a normal woman's voice, so I began to turn around. "No, don't!"

That was the last thing I heard before everything went dark.

Chapter 12

To Stone

I woke up staring into the sky. My body was stiff and I could barely move even a fingertip. I had a sinking suspicion that I'd been turned to stone, but I didn't see any tree tops over me. This was slightly different from what Petros had said. I could finally move my head enough to look around a bit. I saw the top of the cave entrance in my peripheral vision. Then, I heard the voice again.

"I can see that you are finally waking up. I'm hiding behind a rock so that I don't accidentally turn you to stone again. I don't want to hurt you and the petrification thing is not something that I can control. It's part of the curse and I certainly didn't ask for it," said the mystery woman.

"You sound surprisingly normal," I said. Still laying there. I could move my foot back and forth, so that was progress.

"Um, thanks. I would say that I am fairly normal, besides the snakes for hair and ability to turn people to stone when they make eye contact with me," she said.

"Your name wouldn't happen to be Medusa, would it?" I asked. I heard a faint gasp.

"How did you know that?" She asked. I panicked a little because I didn't know how to answer.

"I read about you or someone like you. She also had snakes for hair and could petrify people. In that story, she was a villain, but a bit of a misunderstood one. I always felt a little bit bad about how things turned out for her. She was kind of a victim," I said, still testing the limits of my de-stiffening body.

"How did things turn out for her? And I'm also a victim by the way, though I prefer survivor," said Medusa. She had a strange sadness to her otherwise steady voice.

"Um, someone cut off her head and used it as a weapon. I have no intention of doing that. I was just asked to come see what was turning people to stone, but you don't sound like a monster," I said.

"I appreciate that. For the record, I never wanted to be like this. Those Mythics did this to me. I trusted them and they stabbed me in the back," she said.

"I'd love to know more of your story as I'm no fan of the Mythics myself. I actually think I'm here to take them out of the picture and free people from their tyranny," I said.

"I like you and I will show some trust in you if you are willing to do the same for me," she said.

"Absolutely," I said with a smile. I was able to push my upper body off of the ground and sat up. I didn't quite trust my legs yet.

"Close your eyes and wait there for a moment," she said. She sounded excited to be talking to someone for an extended period. I nodded and closed my eyes. I heard her walk past me and into the mouth of the cave. After about a minute I heard her return and walk behind me. She tied a blindfold on me and I felt her attempt to help lift me off of the ground. "I don't think I can lift you to your feet. I'm pretty strong from moving petrified people, but I couldn't move you at all."

"That makes sense. I'm very large at this point. Would you mind sharing your story with me?" I asked. I was being led over to a log that I sat on when prompted. Medusa sat next to me.

"I used to work in Athena's tribute collection store-house. My parents were both teachers in Erimos, a city on the western coast where the giant statue of

Poseidon is. They fell behind in their tributes and I volunteered to work in the storehouse so that Athena wouldn't get angry and punish them. One day, Poseidon and Athena were visiting and I guess I caught Poseidon's attention. I won't speak of what he did to me, but Athena was incensed and felt it was a violation of the sanctity of her storehouse. She couldn't take her anger out on Poseidon, so she decided to take it out on me. Athena used her knowledge to create a cursed potion. She lied about what it did and offered it as a gift. It turned my hair to snakes to drive people away from me and made it so that looking into my eyes caused the person to turn to stone. Both were to make it impossible for me to have any meaningful friendships or relationships. So far it has certainly done that," she said. I couldn't see her, but I heard her start to cry when she finished speaking. I placed an arm around her and patted her shoulder as gently as possible.

"I'm sorry for what you went through. You didn't deserve any of it," I continued to try and comfort her as she continued to cry. "Those Mythics can't stop us from having a meaningful friendship. At least, I'm willing to be your friend if you'd like. My name is Mae, by the way. The only tribute I'm planning on giving the Mythics is a knuckle sandwich."

She laughed at my lame joke and I felt her wipe her eyes. "I'd like that very much, Mae. Both the friendship and for you to beat them. I really appreciate you listening to my story. This is the most I've spoken to another person since I was banished."

"Is there anything I can do to help you?" I asked.

"You can start with Poseidon and Athena. Also, I'd like to leave this cave area," she said. The sadness had left her voice and it sounded more resolute.

"Deal," I said. "We will probably have to come up with another solution if you want to travel with me. I can't be blindfolded at all times."

"That makes sense," she said.

"Oh, it's nearly nightfall. I have an idea," I said. I called for Noctua as loud as I could, which was quite loud. "Now we wait. Would you mind putting the blindfold on so my owl friend doesn't get petrified when she visits. Or if she visits."

"Sure, that's fine. How is an owl going to help?" She asked. I closed my eyes tightly and she removed the blindfold. After a moment she indicated that she was now wearing it.

"She is an extremely wise owl. Maybe she'll have an idea for us," I explained.

We chatted about life and waited there for about another fifteen minutes before Noctua flew into view.

She landed nearby and did the little owl head tilt at the blindfolded, snake-haired woman beside me.

"If she makes eye contact with anyone, they turn to stone for about a day. I didn't know if it would work on you which is why she is blindfolded currently. I'd like for her to travel with me, but we would need a way to prevent her from petrifying people. Do you have any ideas?" I asked. The owl was silent for a moment and then spoke. Her speech startled Medusa who wasn't expecting it.

"You could try a helmet with a visor or a veil of some sort. It's possible that one of those solutions would keep people from being able to make eye contact and thus solve the problem at hand," she said, then she flew away before I could follow up.

"Thank you," shouted Medusa as the owl flew away.

"Well, those are practical ideas. We probably want to do some testing before being around too many people." I grabbed my backpack and started going through it. "I don't know if I have any fabric that is see through."

"I have something we could try. Close your eyes because I have to take off my blindfold," she said. After a moment she spoke again. "Sorry in advance if this doesn't work, but you can open your eyes when ready."

I opened my eyes and looked at her. Nothing happened. She had taken the blindfold which was just a small piece of cloth, unfolded it, and draped it over her head. It was already fairly dark so the seeing test would probably have to wait until morning, but it was a start.

"Well, I'm not stone. Can you see anything?" I asked.

"Not well, but it is pretty dark out already. Maybe we can use this until we can get to a town with a shop that sells fabric and find something better suited for this," she thought for a moment. "Actually, I don't have any money and basically just have the clothes on my back. I may have to figure out a way to make some drachma before we travel too much."

"Don't worry about that. I've got you covered," I said.

"You've already been nicer to me than anyone else in recent memory. I couldn't let you pay for everything," said Medusa.

"You absolutely can. The last two large monsters I defeated both dropped a coin worth a hundred drachma. I don't need expensive weapons and armor, so I really don't need it that much at this point," I said.

"Thank you, Mae. I'll do what I can to contribute. Maybe we can find a way to use my curse as a blessing," she said.

I chatted with her about what had happened to me over the last week or so, but I didn't talk about my life or the man in white. I didn't know if either of us were ready for that yet. I slept out under the stars and she retired to her cave.

This night of sleep was troubled by a vision of a time when I had invited a couple of my closest friends over for a card game. It was the first and last time that I attempted that. They were very concerned about my husband and his usual way of dealing with whatever was going on in his brain. I was embarrassed and never ended up inviting them back to my house again. Maybe this was subconsciously one of the reasons I felt like such a kindred spirit to Medusa. I also had difficulties with close friendships. Hiding bruises and not being able to take my husband to anything hurt my friendships too. He was kind of like my curse.

I woke up to something shaking me and heard Medusa's voice.

"I think you're having a bad dream," she said. Then everything went dark.

The unfortunate feeling of coming out of the petrified state came over me as I came to.

"I'm so sorry. You were having a bad dream and I tried to wake you up, but the cloth slipped off my head as I shook you and we must've made eye contact accidentally. I'm so sorry!" Medusa's voice came from beside me as I waited for the effects to wear off. "The veil is on. Again, I'm very sorry."

"It was an accident. Everything is okay. We are okay. I would say that we probably need to find a better solution than just draping a cloth over your head. Like maybe make it part of a hat or something," I said.

"As long as it is a soft hat. My snakes are pretty sensitive." She gave them a gentle head pat and I had more questions about snake hair, but thought it wasn't the time.

After a few minutes I was able to get up and stretch out a bit. Medusa didn't have much to travel with so leaving the cave wasn't too difficult. She had a small bag slung over her shoulder and I could see the edge of a blanket sticking out of the top. The bag was woven from some sort of cordage and it looked like she made it herself while she was out here.

"Ready?" I asked.

"Yes. I travel light," said Medusa. She smiled at her comment, but the smile didn't reach her eyes. I could tell she was a little sad, but who wouldn't be in her situation.

"My plan was to head to Lysandria and then catch a boat south to Cythara," I said.

"Why do you want to go there again? That's one of the major hub cities for the Mythics," said Medusa as we began to walk east toward Lysandria.

"I just wanted to hit all the major cities and find some monsters to take care of. I need to get stronger. What do you mean by major hub?" I asked.

"I forget that you're new here. Cythara has the tribute store houses for Aphrodite and Hephaestus. Luckily, the Theogamia Festival has passed. They throw a huge party that celebrates love and supposedly the marriage of Zeus and Hera, but really it's just a drachma-grab for Aphrodite. At least, I think it has passed," she said. Her face adopted a bit of confusion. I guess it would be difficult to keep track of time when you live in a cave for years.

"That sounds kind of like Valentine's Day back where I came from. Everyone buys flowers and candy for each other and gives little cards confessing their love. Stuff like that. I remember getting Valentine's from my husband before the war." I stopped walking and got unexpectedly choked up. It came out of nowhere. I hadn't really thought about Valentine's Day in decades.

"I didn't know you were married," said Medusa. She had also stopped walking and was now looking at me. She must've noticed the sudden shift. "I'm so sorry. Did you lose your husband in that war?"

"I lost the part of him that celebrated Valentine's Day in that war. He died much later, but a part of him was lost." I straightened my shoulders, stood as tall as possible, and continued walking. Medusa thought better than to continue that conversation for now and quickly changed the subject. My towering over her may have been the trigger for her next topic of conversation.

"You are the tallest and most muscled woman I've ever met. How strong are you anyway?"

"I don't know actually. I haven't done a proper test besides lifting logs and fighting monsters." I picked up a stone that sat nearby that was about the size of a softball, maybe a bit larger. I threw it as hard as I possibly could at a tree about twenty or so feet in front of us. The stone rocketed from my hand faster than I thought possible and struck the tree with a solid thunk. The tree was less than a foot wide and the stone had stuck it dead center about waist high up the trunk. The back of the tree splintered out from the force and it began to fall toward us. I saw that I had unlocked a skill called 'Ballistos', but was too focused on the falling tree to want to check it out yet.

I positioned myself between the tree and Medusa and raised my arms to catch it. The middle of the tree landed on the meat of my shoulder, but because I had braced myself I was able to stop its motion completely. I pushed the tree up and tossed it to the side.

"Are you okay?" I said, sheepishly. I didn't mean for that to happen at all and I wasn't sure if any stray branches had whacked my new traveling pal.

"That was amazing! I've never seen strength like that. Did it hurt when the tree fell on your shoulder?" She asked. I guess it was a good question. A normal person would have broken bones or at least suffered some damage from an impact like that.

"Oh, that's the other reason that I'm not scared to take on the Mythics. I'm invincible."

Chapter 13

BLUE FUR

Medusa and I continued walking toward Lysandria while I told her more of my story in this land so far. I told her about the different monsters I'd faced up to this point and how I'd defeated them. She seemed most interested in my Mighty Leap ability and even asked to see it in action.

"Stand back a bit," I said as I squatted down and waited for the skill to be ready. Right when I was about to take off, I caught a glimpse of blue fur ducking behind a tree about twenty feet or so to Medusa's back. I decided to still finish the leap, but change my landing spot just a bit. The maximum height felt much higher than what I'd been able to jump in the past and I figured it was from the level up and the extra points I'd put into strength. I was slightly worried about the height I could achieve if I kept leveling up my strength humor.

I landed with a crash close to where I'd last seen the blue fur and saw the frightened, odd-colored monkeys scatter. They were hooting and hollering at me as they climbed into the surrounding trees. I ran back to Medusa and asked her if she'd seen whatever these things were before.

"They're called kerkopes," she said. "I usually just end up turning them to stone and leaving them in the woods if they wandered too close to my cave. After the first couple of times, they just stayed away from me."

"Are they dangerous?" I asked.

"I don't think so. At least, they've never attacked me before. They might not recognize me with the veil and being so far from my cave. You want me to petrify them?" Medusa asked while pointing to her face.

"No, I think I just scared them pretty good. They probably heard the tree that I destroyed and are just checking us out. They don't seem overly violent and they remind me of what we called monkeys back home," I said. She shrugged and we kept walking. I still heard the monkey-esque noises behind us every once in a while. They seemed to be communicating, but I couldn't understand them. After a few minutes of silence, I felt a tug at my backpack. One of the kerkopes was trying to yank it off of my back.

I swatted its hand away, but it was quick enough to avoid contact. I heard a grunt from Medusa and then a thud like a bowling ball falling to the ground.

"Close your eyes!" I heard her yell. I did immediately, but wasn't sure exactly what had happened. "One tried to steal my veil and it turned to stone and fell to the ground. It still has my veil in its now stone hand."

A cacophony of now angry monkey noises surrounded us. They didn't seem to like one of their buddies getting turned to stone.

"Get behind me and watch my back. If they come your way, petrify them. I'll do what I can to scare them off," I said, picking up a nearby rock.

"Okay, I'm behind you. You can open your eyes, but don't turn around. If you get petrified, I don't know if I can get them all before they overwhelm me," she said.

I threw the rock at a tree that one of the kerkopes was in. It hit the trunk near the branch that the monkey creature was standing on and the branch snapped off. The blue monkey hit the ground with a thud and started making the angry noises.

"How many of these things are there?" I asked.

"I've only ever seen a couple at a time. You must've brought all of them in with how loud that splintering tree was. I've gotten two more so far," she said.

"I think I've seen another ten or so. It's hard to tell with how fast they can move through the trees." I kept picking up anything I could get my hands on and throwing the objects at the quick little beasts. They didn't look as cute now as they bared their fangs at me.

I ran out of rocks and tree limbs to throw, but hadn't actually been able to hit any of them. The only good thing about my constant throwing was that I seemed to be encouraging them to rotate behind me. They weren't the most intelligent of animals and I heard Medusa calling out whenever she turned another one to stone.

"That's six," she said. There was a hint of exhilaration in her voice.

I picked up the monkey statue that had stolen Medusa's veil and attempted to pull the veil out of its tiny stone fist. A fragment of the hand broke off and the veil came loose. I gave the veil to Medusa for safe keeping. Instinctually, I brought the stone Kerkope up into a throwing position and chucked it at another of the little monsters that had gotten a bit too close. The petrified monkey hit the non-stone one with a sickening crunch and they both came to rest at the base of the tree the non-stone one had been in.

The others got even more upset at that and their screams intensified. I was getting a bit worried about Medusa and thought a change of strategy was in order. I pulled up my map and the chaos around me froze. Medusa was facing east and I was facing west. I judged the distance to be within range for us to get out of this forest, but I needed to make sure our exit was clear. I put the map away and time resumed.

"We need to move the direction you're facing until you see a clearing in the trees above you. When you give the signal, crouch down, close your eyes, and cover your head with your hands," I said.

"I don't like the sound of this, but I'll start moving. I don't like these things at all," said Medusa. As she walked, I stayed behind her and kept throwing anything I could get my hands on from the forest floor. I briefly saw a notification after a couple more minutes, but it wasn't a level up notification. Things were too hectic for me to read it and I was too focused on staying with Medusa to care about the message too much at the moment.

"Okay, there's a clearing. I'm closing my eyes and crouching as soon as I stop speaking," she said. I turned and squatted down. I pulled her into my arms and tried to protect as much of her as possible as I'd never tried anything like this before. I used Mighty

Leap and the two of us shot up through the clearing. My target was the clearing to the east of us on my map. We landed about halfway between the edge of the forest and Lysandria and I gently set Medusa down. My eyes were still shut tight.

"I didn't enjoy that experience at all," she said. "I suppose it was better than the kerkopes though."

"Are you okay?" I asked.

"Yes and I have my veil back on now too," she said.

I remembered that a notification had briefly shown and pulled up my menus to see if I could locate it. I didn't see anything new on my main menu that showed my level and humors. When I swapped over to my skills menu, the notification was still listed at the top of the screen. I read the message.

> You have leveled up the skill Ballistos from 'Apraxos' to 'Metrios'.

Once I'd read the message, it disappeared from the top of the screen. I looked down the list of skills to find the new one that had already leveled up from me constantly throwing things for an extended period of time during that fight. It would be a very handy skill indeed.

> Ballistos (Metrios)
> You can imbue up to five Energy Points (EP) into any thrown objects. The force of the object's impact is multiplied by 10% for each EP imbued.

"Medusa, could you tell me what 'Apraxos' and 'Metrios' means?" I asked. I didn't recognize those words at all. My back up plan was to call for Noctua later and ask her, but I figured that it didn't hurt to ask.

"I've heard those terms before. They are usually used when people are trying to learn something new or develop a trade skill. 'Apraxos' has to do with being untrained or without any experience like a natural starting point and 'Metrios' is when you have gained some competence. It isn't perfect, but it shows growth in that area," she explained. It immediately made me wonder if my other skills would be leveling up at some point and what the level after 'Metrios' was. Would I get special perks every time I grew in skill? I was excited to put this newly upgraded skill to the test.

I found a nearby stone and focused on putting EP into it. The action was intuitive and once completed, I hurled the stone towards the forest. I could feel the extra power in the throw and the stone sailed away like a cannonball. I saw the forest canopy shake momentarily. Evidence of an innocent tree trunk having been hit by the projectile.

"Yeah, that could do some damage," I said. "Let's get to town before I attract any other monsters though. We need to get you a better head covering. Can you imagine if you accidentally petrified me during a big fight? I don't think that would be good for either of us."

"I agree completely," she said.

We could see the town of Lysandria in the distance. She shared about her family and about life growing up in Erimos while we walked. I could hear the sadness in her voice as she spoke and I found myself getting more and more angry with the Mythics for their abuses. The unhealthy power dynamic also reminded me of my marriage. The realization further cemented my desire to take them down. I wished that I could've done more to protect my son, David, from his father. Thinking back, I didn't really see any alternatives to our situation. We didn't have any other family to speak of and I was too embarrassed to ask friends for help.

Medusa's soft words broke me out of my thoughts. "Are you okay?"

"Yeah, I was just thinking about my late husband," I said, cementing resolve on my face.

"You must really hate him," she said. Her assessment of my relationship with him hit me hard.

"I should, shouldn't I. Hate makes the most sense with what he put us through," I said, continuing to stare forward toward my goal.

"You seem to hold a lot of strong, negative feelings toward the man," said Medusa, matching my speed.

"That I do, but even now, I couldn't say that I hate him. In fact, I think the negative emotions might be so strong because of how much I loved him. The first part of our relationship was like a dream and I fell so hard for him. Head over heals in love is the saying where I come from. I don't think I ever hated him, no matter how much he hurt me. Isn't that strange?" I asked.

"It is a bit strange, to be honest. I guess love doesn't always make sense," she said.

Chapter 14

SNAKE HAIR

We arrived in Lysandria and went into the general goods store called 'The Talaria'. I figured that this was as good a place as any to begin our search for a head covering. I waved over at the shopkeeper and he approached with a smile.

"Good morning," I said, matching his smile.

"Good morning. Welcome to 'The Talaria'. I'm Tychon, the keeper of this shop. What can I help you with this fine day?" He asked. He was in his forties or fifties, it was difficult to tell. He was a bit round about the middle, but he had a hidden strength in him. He was probably a father, they have strange dad strength.

"We're looking for a veil of some sort that will fit around her head better without falling off," I said, motioning over to Medusa. She did look a bit odd with a piece of fabric draped over her head.

"I see," said Tychon. He took a step toward Medusa and his face showed that he was studying her situation and trying to piece it together. He was obviously struggling to understand why this young woman had a cloth over her head. Medusa broke the increasingly awkward silence.

"I have a condition where looking another person or creature in the eye makes them immediately turn to stone," she said as matter-a-factly as one could. Tychon took a step back, but then caught himself.

"I understand, young lady. I think I can help you," he said as the big, reassuring smile came back to his face after its brief vacation. "Everyone is a bit different, eh? But that's what makes the world interesting."

I could see Medusa smiling from underneath the veil. Tychon was either a slick businessman or, what seemed more likely, he was just a good man. It's possible that he had a daughter our age and he just knew what to say to be helpful.

"Excuse me for a moment, ladies. I'll be right back with some options." He disappeared into the back of the store and various noises could be heard that indicated searching for and shuffling of objects was taking place. After about ten or fifteen minutes spent in mindless browsing, he returned. He laid out the items he had found on the main counter and motioned us over in a friendly 'I'm-ready-when-you-are' sort of way.

"Thank you for your help, Tychon," said Medusa as we approached the counter.

"Of course! What kind of shop keeper would I be if I didn't try my best to help everyone who came through my doors?" He asked rhetorically. He motioned over the items he had laid out on the counter. "I think one of these options should do the trick."

Medusa picked up and inspected each option one by one. There was a thin veil, like what a bride might have worn. It had a hair clip and hairpin to hold it in place. This wouldn't work with the snake hair. She passed over two more thicker veils that had similar, non-snake hair friendly attachment methods. The last option was what looked like a bee-keeper's hat with a chin strap to attach it. She picked it up, but remembered the danger.

"Please, close your eyes for a moment, both of you," said Medusa. Tychon looked at me and I nodded at him that it would be a good idea to comply. Once our eyes were closed, we waited for the all clear. Which came a few moments after the request was initially made. "It's perfect."

We both instinctively opened our eyes to look at the end result. The wide-brimmed hat fit perfectly over the snakes and if you didn't know they were there, you wouldn't even know they were snakes through the veil. She demonstrated vigorously moving her head around to show how well the chin strap held the hat in place. I was nervous, but trusted her. The veil stayed in place as it was a little on the thicker side, but she said that she could see through it just fine. If she physically lifted the veil, she could still utilize her power, but she didn't test that here.

"We'll take this one," I said to the shop keeper.

"That will be three drachma," said Tychon. I handed over the money and shook his hand. Medusa was beaming that everything had worked out so nicely. She also looked relieved that she wouldn't have to worry so much about accidental petrifications in the future. We said our goodbyes and left the store happy.

The next leg of our journey would take us to Cythara so we needed to find a boat. We walked over to the port area of town and began our search. The ports were mostly empty of ships. It made sense that most of them would've left early in the morning for the day's catch. There was one smaller vessel toward the end of the dock that had a person on it so we headed that way.

"Hello!" Yelled Medusa as we approached the lone sailor. He turned from the net mending that he was currently engrossed in and greeted us with a wave.

"Do you take charters, sir?" I asked when we got close enough for a regular conversation.

"I'd have to ask the captain. I'm new to his crew and I'm not sure what his protocol is on things of that sort," said the man. He stepped over to the edge of the ship and looked us over with a bit of hesitation. "He should be back soon. My name is Delmar and the Captain is Galen."

"Nice to meet you, Delmar. My name is Mae and this is Medusa. You said you're new to his crew. Did you just move to the area?" I said, trying to kill some time until the captain returned.

"It's nice to meet you as well. No, I've lived in Lysandria my whole life and I've been a fisherman my whole life. My last vessel was attacked by the monster that I hear was recently defeated. There was a big party and the town eating the monster made me feel a little better about the attack. I'm just sad I was still recovering and couldn't make it to the party. Captain Galen took me on as some extra help."

"Well, I'm glad you were able to find a new position so quickly. The monster was surprisingly delicious. I'm sorry you missed it," I said.

"I'm just glad to be back on my feet," he said. His face showed a strange sadness mixed with a smile. He must've really thought that he was done for. "How long have you been in town?"

"Oh, I came when the monster was defeated. So not too long ago," I said.

"That's lucky. You came to town just in time. That monster was huge and really had the town, especially sailors, living in fear," he said.

"She was the one who killed the monster," said Medusa. "She's just being modest."

The sailor's eyes went wide and shot over to me. "That was you?"

"It was. It attacked me on the beach when I first visited the southern coast here. I was looking for a vessel to take me to Cythara," I said, as calm and cool as possible.

"Thank you for killing that thing. It took out so many fishing boats and many of my friends were lost," he said as he hopped over to the pier and took my hand to shake it. I stood about a foot taller than the sailor and he took notice now that we were on equal footing. "It's no wonder that you could kill that monster. You're massive."

"That doesn't seem like a nice thing to say to a lady," I said, feigning a bit of offence. The sailor immediately bowed down a bit and moved his forehead toward the back of my hand that he was still holding.

"I'm so sorry, Mae. I meant no offence. I just meant that you're very powerful," said Delmar.

"I was just playing. You're fine. I know that I'm very large." I gave a gentle tug on my hand and he released it and took a step back. His head was still slightly bowed.

After a moment of awkward silence, he cleared his throat and jumped back over to the boat. "The captain should be back soon."

We spent spent time staring out at the water and listening to the lapping waves in silence while we waited for the captain. After a while we heard a voice from behind us.

"Hello, ladies! I hear that you'd like a ride to Cythara." We turned to see a man in what could only have been a captain's hat. "I'm Captain Galen and I do take on charters, if the price is right."

"Thank you so much Captain Galen. What would be the right price for a charter to Cythara?" I asked.

"Twenty drachma will get you there," said the Captain with a smile.

"Does that sound high to you, Medusa? I don't really know what a good price is," I said.

"Maybe a bit high, but I've never had to get a charter before," said Medusa.

"I can assure you that twenty drachma per charter guest is a standard rate when the waters are this full of monsters," said the Captain.

"Well, if I can fight one big monster when we get to Cythara, I'll get another hundred drachma. I'll still have made gains, so it's a deal," I said. I handed over the forty drachma and the captain snapped into action. He jumped on his ship and began shouting orders. Another crewman came from below decks and began completing the various boat-related tasks. I didn't know many of the boat terms, but they looked to be working hard. After about fifteen or so minutes of furied movement on the main deck the captain called us aboard.

We hopped onto the ship and the anchor was raised. As we pulled away from the dock a feeling of unease began to make my mind question the decision of heading out on the water. I still didn't know if I could drown or would I just sink to the bottom and have to try and figure out which way to start walking. Both were terrifying concepts. The captain must've noticed the worry on my face as my brain ran through the possible scenarios.

"We do have some protection from the monsters," he said, pointing to the small cannons at the front and back of the ship. I hadn't even been thinking about the monsters. The cannons were maybe half of the size of the cannons I'd seen in movies. I could easily lift these if I'd wanted to. The large stack of baseball sized cannon balls didn't instill any more confidence either.

"I'm more scared of drowning then of being attacked, I think," I said, honestly trying to assess where I was landing on the subject.

"I have the perfect solution then," said the captain. He scuttled down into the hold and popped back out a few minutes later. He was carrying something that I didn't recognize because it didn't look much like the modern iteration. "Do you mind if I outfit you for the voyage?"

"Go ahead if you think it'll help," I said. After a few minutes of buckling and tying, I was ready. Honestly, it did make me feel a little better. Medusa's giggles didn't though. I guess I did look a little ridiculous. I now had an ill-fitting vest of wooden slats buckled around me. The wood was light and looked a little like sheets of thick cork shoved into rectangular pouches. I looked a little like an adult wearing a kid-sized life jacket since I'm so large. This added to Medusa's amusement.

Seeing her standing there in her bee-keeper's hat and looking down at my too-small, wooden life vest, I couldn't help but laugh along with her. What a strange situation I was in.

An hour or so had passed with the two of us killing time by leaning over the rear railing and watching the movement of the water. It was amazingly relaxing and I honestly had no idea how long we'd been staring in silence. It was so peaceful. That's when I saw it. Something under the water that was large, serpentine, and moving faster than the ship.

"Did you see that?" I asked Medusa who snapped out of her peaceful stupor.

"See what?" Asked Medusa.

"I don't know, but it was big. Be ready to brace yourself against this railing, just in case this feeling in my gut is right." I moved over to where the Captain was and told him what I'd seen. His eyes went wide.

"All hands! We have a ketos! Prepare for battle!" He shouted these instructions, his crew got to their places behind the small cannons, and then the deck went dead silent. The sound of the water hitting the sides of the vessel went from a calming experience to a rhythmic reminder that we didn't know exactly what was below the waves. We also didn't know when or if it would attack. Seconds turned to minutes and everyone on deck began looking back and forth between each other and the captain as if to ask what to do next.

"What's a ketos?" I asked the captain in a whisper as the threat of attack seemed to lessen.

"Sea monster," he whispered back. He then put a finger to his lips then switched to two fingers scanning the horizon. The message to quietly look for threats was clear and I followed them. After another minute, I felt safe to venture some words.

"I swear I saw something," I whispered to the captain who was still next to me. I was beginning to doubt myself though. Had my eyes deceived me?

That's when I heard a scream. It was Medusa. She was to my right across the ship's deck. She was sitting on the deck and holding onto the railing for dear life with one arm while the other arm was pointed behind me. I turned to see three fish-snake hybrid heads gently swaying from side to side above long, slender necks. It reminded me of what the Loch Ness monster was supposed to look like, but with three heads.

"Fire!" Shouted the captain with steely resolve. The cannons fired in quick succession with none of the shots connecting. It turns out that hitting a moving target, or three, that were only a foot or so across while also moving wasn't easy. The monster roared and came further out of the water. A clawed, three fingered hand came out of the water as well. The hand that reminded me of a dragon's grabbed the closest gunner, tossed him into the air as if he weighed nothing, and caught him with one of the heads.

The sailor's struggling ceased with a sickening crunch from the powerful jaws.

The fight for our lives was on. Well, the fight for their lives was on. I'd probably be okay. I instantly felt bad for thinking that.

Chapter 15

THE KETOS

I picked up one of the baseball sized cannonballs and mentally activated Ballistos. I only added one Energy Point, which was the minimum, since I wasn't sure if I'd even be able to hit this thing. I flung the heavy ball at the monster's central head and the ball connected with a loud crack. I wished that I'd dumped more EP into the throw, but the center head probably at least had a pretty bad headache. A fractured skull tends to have that effect.

While the central head looked dazed and confused, the other two heads looked focused and angry. Unfortunately, they were both focused on me. The heads struck with lightning speed as I felt myself being lifted from the ship's deck. The left head had my right arm and shoulder in it's razor sharp maw while the right head had my left leg and was thrashing it about.

They played tug-o-war with my invincible body like two dogs fighting over a bone. It was the strangest feeling, but I wasn't taking any damage. Right head won its prize with one final jerk. The head attempted to bite me into swallowable pieces since I was much larger than the first unfortunate sailor. After a few minutes that I could've only imagined were frustrating for the monster, it changed tactics and whipped me toward the boat. I went flying and struck the side of the vessel with a thud.

I quickly scrambled up the side of the ship and pulled myself over the railing and back onto the main deck. The central head was back in the fight and all three looked at me briefly as if assessing their next move. The captain was at the cannon that had become gunnerless and fired a shot at the back of the monster that was just barely breaking the water's surface. The cannonball smacked off the hard scales that covered the monster's back, but it was enough to make the captain a target.

I guessed the monster's next move based on the heads turning their focus onto the captain. I was already in motion when the central head swung down to bite the man who'd been nice enough to take us aboard. I caught its open jaws with one of my massive hands on the top set of teeth and another on the bottom set. The teeth that would have ripped right through normal fingers couldn't hurt mine, but they did provide a reasonable amount of grip, so I could hold on tight. I was using all my strength trying to rip this set of jaws apart and take them out of the fight. Like trying to open a bear trap, but not in a smart way under normal circumstances.

I wasn't strong enough to rip the jaws apart, but I could put a lot of force against the jaws. The monster had been using all of its strength in an attempt to close its mouth and bite my fingers off. It wasn't expecting me to just let go. When I released my grip and the jaws snapped closed, it had to have done damage. The sudden full force jaw snap seemed to have hurt as this set of eyes had closed in what I could only describe as a pained expression. Like when you bite your tongue. While this head recovered, I clasped my fists together and brought them down as hard as I could right between its eyes. The head started to slide toward the side of the boat and looked unconscious.

As the central head slid over the railing, Delmar sliced through its neck where it was thinnest. The timing was perfect and the lifeless neck slipped overboard and into the water while the head stayed aboard. The other two heads didn't like this very much at all based on the monstrous roar they emitted.

Left head redoubled its efforts fighting crew that were doing a great job of defending themselves with swords and makeshift clubs.

Right head decided to get revenge on Delmar and moved to strike. I dove for the head as soon as I saw the attack start, but with the monster's speed, I was only able to catch it around the neck instead of being able to repeat my last move. Delmar's sword was quick enough to slow the head's attack and with me around its neck, I was the new threat to worry about. Revenge could wait.

The right head shot up into the air with me still holding on for dear life. I was hugging the neck right at the top near the monster's head and was now directly over the massive body of the ketos. I loosened my grip enough to slide down the neck until I landed on the main body in a squatted position. I still had the right neck in my grip though it was quite a bit thicker at the base. My arms barely fit around it. I squeezed with all my strength and activated Mighty Leap as soon as I was able to. My grip held true with the scales of the monster helping secure my arms in place. Myself and the neck separated from the body of the beast and landed back on the deck of the ship.

I released my grip and the neck hit the main deck folding in on itself before sliding to a stop against the rails opposite the monster. Two down and one to go. The last one seemed to be the smart one as it had sent the others into the most dangerous situations, or maybe it was just the lucky one. Whatever the case may be, it was definitely the angry one. The final head decided to try a different approach, maybe a more desperate one. It bit down on me and flung me into the water behind it as hard as it could. I didn't really get a say in the matter as it happened so fast.

My funny looking life vest worked perfectly. I bobbed there in the water with my head above the surface. No drowning for me. It was great at keeping me afloat, but not so great at allowing me to swim quickly. I saw the monster grab another sailor, bite him in half, and toss the uneaten half into the water. I hoped it wasn't Delmar or Galen, but it was bad no matter who it was. I tried to swim as quickly as possible toward the ship, but after struggling to make good progress quickly, I had a decision to make.

I ripped the life vest off and swam as quickly as my powerful body could move. I was able to move much faster this way and reached the tail end of the sea monster in probably thirty seconds. I grabbed the tail and climbed onto its back. It didn't want a repeat of the neck ripping incident and quickly rolled me off of its back and into the water beside it. I felt a clawed hand grasp me and my biggest fear was realized.

It held me underwater as I attempted to peel its clawed fingers back enough for me to escape its grasp. As I got one finger up, the other hand grasped me as well. I wasn't going anywhere. I guess it was time to figure out this whole drowning question. Being underwater like this was a weird sensation. My many decades on Earth had trained me into thinking I needed to breath, but the fact that I'd been submerged for a good while and didn't seem to be bothered by the lack of oxygen was a reassuring dichotomy.

I felt such a feeling of relief until everything began to go dark. I wasn't blacking out though. No, I was sinking. Oh no. I was starting to panic when the fingers that held me began to feel less pliable. They didn't have any give. That's when I realized that the sea monster had been turned to stone. I was able to break the fingers off now with some effort, but the amount of ambient light was still fading. This thing was still sinking, but it would just unpetrify in a day and be back to hurting people again. Plus, I wanted my hundred drachma. I was able to grab the last neck as it sank past me. I was able to hold onto the neck and kick at the head until it separated.

I received some notifications, but didn't want to pause time by getting into my menus to read them while underwater. With the last bit of light, I was able to see the glint of the coin over the center of the monster. I pulled myself over to it and put it into my inventory. That's when I saw the rope. There was a harpoon with a rope attached stuck into the back of the sea monster. I quess this was the type of implement you'd find on a fishing vessel, but I hadn't expected it. I grabbed the harpoon and yanked it out of the stone monster's back like some weird version of excalibur.

I began swim-climbing the rope and felt more and more positive as the amount of light increased. It took me a few minutes to break the surface and the sailors cheered as they pulled me up on deck. Medusa ran over and gave me a hug.

"I'm so sorry. I knew the ketos had grabbed you, so I shouldn't have turned it to stone." She squeezed harder and it felt nice to have a friend here that really cared about me.

"You were in an intense situation and I'm sure you did what you had to do. It actually ended up helping me because I couldn't break the fingers until they were petrified. Who knows how long I would've been trapped underwater if you hadn't turned the monster to stone," I said, trying to reassure her.

She released her death grip and looked up at me. "Being trapped underwater like that must've been scary. Were you holding your breath the whole time?"

I smiled down at her because this fight took away one of my biggest fears. I whispered to her so as not to let any of the sailors overhear this part. "I learned that I can't drown. I don't quite understand the power in this world that makes me invincible, but it was like a switch was flipped when I went underwater and I just didn't need to breath. It was odd, but empowering."

The sailors were quickly moving around the deck. Some were fixing a rip in the sail, others were busily tying ropes and doing other support activities. One man was staring at the massive monster neck that was still laying on the deck where I'd dropped it. I walked over and stared at it with him. "What are you thinking?"

"I was thinking about how to cook this thing. There's a lot of good meat on that neck and the lads would probably love a change of pace from the fish we eat constantly," said the man. He had a large knife and a barrel next to him. As he leaned down and started to cut off chunks of meat, I decided that it was time for me to go somewhere else. I could never have been a butcher.

I went back over by Medusa who was leaning over the back railing and watching the water in peace. I joined her and we watched together in silence for a while. I remembered something from the fight that I'd been curious about. "I forgot to ask who threw the harpoon with the rope attached to it? That thing helped me feel a bit better about being so far underwater as I still felt a bit of connection to the ship."

"That was Captain Galen. The ketos had focused on me and when it's last head came close enough, I lifted my veil and petrified it. The head, then the neck, then the body all turned to stone and the captain landed that harpoon just before the back turned to stone. I think he was trying to help you," she said.

"I'll have to thank him for that." I had another realization. I'd gotten some more notifications. Medusa must've noticed the excited look on my face.

"What's going on?" She asked.

"That fight made me stronger," I said. I went into my menus and saw the notification about the monster being defeated. The other notification was about leveling up. I put all my points into Melanc as I just felt like I needed to be stronger. I read my stats and felt pretty good about the extra power.

Mae June Cohen

Level 4 - Kolossos

HP - 130/130

EP - 93/400

---

5   Sanguin: This humor has a direct correlation to constitution and HP.

7   Coleric: This humor has a direct correlation to speed and agility.

5   Flegmat: This humor has a direct correlation to intellect and luck.

32 Melanc: This humor has a direct correlation to strength and EP.

Medusa's eyes went wide when I jumped out of the menu and time unfroze. I'd grown a few inches taller and my muscles had also grown. "Are you even bigger?"

"Probably," I said nonchalantly. I smiled at her and flexed my slightly larger arms. She rolled her eyes. We watched the water as the sun set. Captain Galen walked over to us after a while. I hadn't bothered him as he had lost men and was yelling out all the commands needed to get the ship ready.

"I've got an area below decks set up for you if you'd like to sleep for a bit. We should be docking in Cythara in the morning now that the sail is repaired," he said. He motioned for us to follow him and we did.

As we walked toward the hatch that led below deck, I saw him giving me an appraising look.

"Yes, I've gotten bigger," I said.

"Sorry, miss. I didn't mean to stare. You're just very impressive. Also, forgive me for not thanking you earlier. We would've lost more men and maybe even the ship if not for the two of you," said the captain. There was a somber sadness that showed how much he cared for the crew he had lost. He tried to hand us back our charter fare that I'd paid, but I refused.

"We were glad to help and you're still getting us to Cythara, so I want you to keep the drachma," I said. We'd arrived at our sleeping quarters and the captain bowed and left us. Medusa looked comfortable in her bed. I looked like a cartoonishly large person trying to sleep in a toddler bed.

"Good night," said Medusa.

"Good night," I said back to her as I drifted into a yet another troubled sleep.

Chapter 16

CELEBRATE LOVE

I stood in the kitchen of our quaint little starter home. David was playing in the next room. Toy soldiers or something like that. The radio was on, but it was just background noise. I had just finished peeling some apples for a pie and starting to feel like there could be hope for normalcy. The American dream for every family whose loved one made it back from fighting over seas. That's all I wanted.

My husband, Felix, sat at the small table with a half cup of black coffee that he'd been sipping while trying to find something fitting to do for work in the local newspaper. These were the moments I cherished. The calm before the storm that I'd wish would be the last. We lie to ourselves a lot for the sake of love.

This peaceful, calm Felix was the one I remembered first falling for. He had such a strong presence, and the kindest eyes. These days his eyes would often just stare out into the distance as if he was a million miles from his wife and child. This turned into one of those times. Halfway through his coffee, he sat the paper down and just stared straight ahead. There wasn't anything interesting on that wall of the kitchen. Maybe he's just enjoying the radio show was the lie I had the clear recollection of telling myself. I knew he had slipped away again. Back to the war.

That's when his breathing changed. Quick and shallow like he was running a marathon in his mind and his body was trying to keep pace. His eyes would flicker and an arm or leg would twitch.

"Are you feeling okay, Felix?" I asked. I waited too many agonizing seconds for an answer that wouldn't come.

A loud noise on the radio was the final straw. Felix's eyes darted around the room. It was like I wasn't there. He was somewhere else now. I felt the knot in my stomach. My motherly instinct was to go to David in the other room, to protect him. I looked and David was still turned the other way, busily playing without a care in the world. It'd be better for him if he didn't even notice the spell his father was having. I chose to stay where I was at and hoped for the best.

The hope didn't hold out. Another shift and the chair that Felix had been sitting in was clattering loudly to the floor. He was in a wide and ready stance. David turned to the kitchen from the noise, but I motioned for him to stay where he was. He didn't want to stay. He wanted to protect me. No kid should have to feel that way, but especially not one under ten years old.

"David, go play in the backyard. I'll come get you in a bit," I said in my mother voice. I was trying to be warm, but commanding. I had to repeat myself before he complied. I remembered being glad he did.

I turned back to Felix who was now shifting uncomfortably looking for threats. He heard the back door close behind David.

"They're coming," he muttered, his voice low and strained, not directed at anyone in particular.

"That was just your son, David, going outside to play. The only other person in this house is me. It's me, your wife, Mae. We're in our home. There aren't any threats," I said. There was a hint of desperation in my voice. I didn't know what would help him get through this.

"They're coming," he said again, stronger this time. I could hear the fear and anger in his voice and it gave me the chills.

Felix turned and picked up the paring knife from the cutting board. He was holding it, ready to strike.

His knuckles were white. "They won't get me. I'm going home!"

"You are home!" I shouted at him. His eyes locked onto mine and for a moment he advanced. My heart pounded in my chest as the fear response took hold. I wanted to run, but I couldn't move. He was within range and I was afraid of what might happen if I made any sudden movements. All my thoughts went to David and what would happen if he was left with only his father to care for him.

The look of raw fear and anger on Felix's face was like that of a cornered animal's desperation. Felix stared at me with eyes that I'd never seen before. I began to cry as the knife raised slightly.

"Felix? It's me. It's Mae. I love you and you love me," I said, not knowing if these would be my last words.

Then, just as suddenly as it had began, all the tension drained from his body. His eyes blinked and softened. They were welling with tears. His gaze went from me, his terrified wife, to the small knife in his hand and it clattered to the ground.

He sank to the ground choking back sobs. By the time I reached the back door to check on David, I could hear Felix lamenting in the kitchen. I'd never heard him cry like that and I hoped that I'd never have to hear it again.

David and I stayed out in the backyard for a while until we saw a composed Felix standing at the back door. I knew he was sorry, but he never said it. That fact almost bothered me more than the incident itself. I'd never look at that knife the same way again. I eventually had to throw it away as each time I saw it in the drawer, I was reminded of that terrible day.

"Land ho!" Yelled a sailor from some unknown location above me. It was enough to wake us both up and Medusa saw the concern on my face.

"Are you okay?" She asked.

"Just another nightmarish memory from my previous life," I explained.

"I'm sorry, Mae. It must've been terrible," she said softly.

"It was. Coincidentally, it helped me to remember why I hate knives." I got up and stretched. Medusa was a good enough friend to not ask anymore questions and just allow me to process things for a few minutes. We went to join the rest of the crew on the main deck. As we climbed the stairs with Medusa just a few steps above me, I told her what was on my heart. "I just really don't want to think about my marriage for a while."

Medusa stopped at the top of the stairs for a brief moment as if her brain broke or she forgot what she was doing. She resumed her climb into the early morning sun and made a comment that I didn't enjoy. "I think it may be a little difficult to not think about marriage."

"What? Why?" I asked as I joined her on the main deck.

"I was wrong about the date. We didn't miss the Theogamia Festival. I think they are just finishing getting it set up," said Medusa.

I couldn't believe my eyes. Strips of pink and red fabric were being hung between the buildings. Vendors were setting up carts with little presents and candies to sell. The festival that celebrated the marriage of Zeus and Hera was about to start and I was stuck on an island with everyone celebrating love and marriage.

This has got to be some sort of sick joke from the man in white or something. There's no way that my luck is this bad. Most of the sailors had already left the ship and headed for the town square, but the captain was still on board.

"Captain Galen, is there any way we could sail somewhere else?" I asked.

"Sorry, Mae. I already released the crew and told them to be back aboard as soon as the festival was over. There's plenty of fun to be had even if you don't buy into the celebration part of the festival," said the captain.

"Where is this ship headed to when the festival is over?" I asked the captain.

"We're just going back to Lysandria. You're welcome to join us, but this time as honorary crew. That means that I wouldn't accept a charter fare, not that I'd make you work. Honestly, we'd all just feel pretty good about having someone as strong as you on board," said Captain Galen.

"I don't know what our plans are yet, but I appreciate the offer. I'll let you know one way or the other. Thanks again for getting us here." I stuck out my massive hand and the captain took it and gave it a shake. It looked like he was shaking hands with a bunch of bananas. I don't think I'll ever get used to being this size. I smiled down at the man who would've towered over me when I was a regular-sized woman back on Earth.

Medusa and I decided to walk around the still peaceful city before the chaos began. Cythara looked like a wealthy city in both old world construction and cleanliness. It's what I had imagined Ancient Rome looking like in its prime. The columns all had the red and pink fabric decorations though, which took away from their beauty to me. I kind of wanted to stick around after all this festival nonsense was cleaned up and see what it would be like without it looking as if Aphrodite had thrown up all over it.

I looked over at Medusa when I saw her arm move. She had tried to secretly wipe a tear from her eyes, but I caught it. "What's wrong?"

"I guess I didn't realize how hard this would hit me. I'll never experience this festival or celebrate love like I used to." Medusa walked over to a nearby set of steps and sat down, crying.

"Everyone has issues, Medusa. That doesn't mean that they can't find love or experience true love. When we first met, you said something about not being able to have meaningful friendships again. I think that you are probably a better friend than I've had in decades and maybe even my whole previous life. Why do you think we became friends so quickly?" I asked the still crying women.

"Because we're both survivors?" She answered with uncertainty.

"I think that is part of it, but that doesn't define you. I think we have become good friends so quickly because you are a wonderful person and people are naturally drawn to wonderful people," I said.

She wiped her eyes and gave me a big smile. "Do you really think I could find someone who could love me, snakes and all?"

"I think so, but I think he will find you. Just call it a mother's intuition," I said. I could tell that she was feeling a lot better. She stood up confidently and wiped her face one last time.

"A big city like this is bound to have some good food options, don't you think?" She asked, changing the subject.

"Absolutely," I said. We turned to continue walking down the streets that were becoming increasingly decorated and increasingly filled with people.

We walked around for probably another hour or so. The city was laid out like a large donut with what would probably be a four lane street making a circle in the center of buildings on both sides. The docks were on the northern side of the island, the western side had the storehouse for Aphrodite, the southern side was all large palatial estates, and the eastern side had Hephaestus's storehouse.

There was a bakery that also made pita like sandwiches and they smelled better than anything else we had passed. We stopped and got some food. Then, we ate while watching all the people in the street walking fast as their feet could take them. Everyone seemed to be so busy here. Even the lovebirds who were holding hands and making googly eyes at each other walked as is they were late for something. All this love was making me a bit annoyed. Maybe it was the bad memories that I had continued having about my late husband or maybe I was a bit upset at the man in white for making me relive all the things that I had wanted to forget.

"I need to fight something," I said, still staring forward towards the street.

"What?" Asked Medusa. "Where'd that come from?"

"I think I'm going to try and find the mayor or whoever's in charge around here and see if they need any monsters defeated," I said, ignoring the questions. "You can just enjoy the festivities."

"I think I'd rather stick with you if that's okay. That's what friends are for. Plus, we already know who's in charge. Aphrodite and Hephaestus run Cythara together," she said.

"That makes sense, I guess. With their storehouses being here," I said. Then, I stopped for a moment and thought about my ultimate goal of freeing people from the tyranny of the Mythics. "I just realized that I've never actually met a Mythic before."

"You'll be fine. They may be tall and intimidating to me, but not for someone powerful and invincible. In my experience, they are two-faced jerks who only care about their own best interests. I wouldn't trust them as far as I could throw them. Although, you could probably throw them pretty far, so I'd trust them less than that in your case," she smiled at her little joke as we kept walking. "We could probably wait for them along the road from their houses. I'd imagine that they'd be joining the festival pretty soon."

We walked back to the road that led to the city from the large estates. We didn't have to wait long to see a large procession coming towards us and it was a sight to behold. Once they were closer, we could see more details about the over-the-top convoy.

First, there were a dozen young ladies on one side of the road and a dozen young men on the other. They were all good-looking, dressed in white with pink trim, and carrying large baskets with a strap over their shoulder. Next came a couple large men dressed in military type armor. The armor was all red and pink with a large heart on the shield. I laughed as they passed which earned a glare from the occupants in the next part of the procession. Two white horses painted with little hearts pulled a chariot with two large individuals. A man and a women. These were the first

Mythics that I'd ever seen and they were admittedly more intimidating than I had thought they'd be.

They were both looking down their noses at me with a sneer and glare that was truly Mythic. I guess I shouldn't have laughed at their procession, but I didn't really care. The stark contrast of what followed them was striking. A jet black carriage pulled by two black horses followed another set of the armored men. This was the end of the procession and it seemed so out of place. It startled me when it stopped right next to us and the door opened.

"Get in," said a deep voice inside the carriage. I got in first and saw the unnaturally shadowed back of the carriage where the voice came from. He spoke again when Medusa began to step up. "Not you."

At this, I began to get up to leave. "I'm not going anywhere without her."

"Stop," said the voice. I took another step toward the exit. "You would defy a Mythic's direct order?"

"A Mythic's orders mean very little to me," I said boldly.

"Excellent," said the voice as a body fully materialized in the shadows.

Chapter 17

THEOGAMIA FESTIVAL

"Please, join us," the shadowy figure said to Medusa. "I apologize for any slight. I'd love to have both of you join me for the parade." Medusa climbed into the carriage and sat down with me across from the massive figure who was sitting in the back. He was about the same size as me, but he had a strange shadowy glow about him. Like a greyish aura. "You may be asking yourself why I stopped. I actually thought for a moment that there was a Mythic that I hadn't met before, but that isn't the case is it?"

His gaze was intense and it took me a moment to gather myself to answer.

"No, I'm not a Mythic. I guess I'd just be called an adventurer. I've been killing monsters and getting stronger," I said.

"I know what you really are and I'd like to partner with you. My name is Hades. Please, tell me more about yourself," he said.

"My name is Mae and this is Medusa. Wait, what do you mean that you know what I really am?" I asked.

"You're a hero and I believe that you're here for a reason, Mae. I saw you laugh in front of Aphrodite and Hephaestus. Do you know how many people would show that kind of disrespect?" Asked Hades. He smiled a strangely mischievous smile.

"A hero? And you seem happy that I don't care about Mythics. What's that all about?" I asked.

"You are most definitely a hero, Mae," he said before his demeanor shifted a bit and he looked frustrated. "I'm no fan of the other Mythics and I've been waiting for a revolution. I'm not in a position to overthrow my brothers and their friends, but I think you can help me take them down a notch. What do you think?"

"I don't know what to think. This seems to be out of place coming from a Mythic," I said, pushing back a bit to try and work out his true intentions.

"I can understand your hesitation and I don't mind laying my cards out on the table before asking you to trust me. My brothers, Zeus and Poseidon, both lord their acclaim and positions over me. I have arguably the worst area of influence compared to the other Mythics. I have the keys to the underworld, but garner the least respect and people even hate me. I'm not the one that makes people die. Realistically, I've probably killed the fewest number of humans out of all of the other Mythics." He paused and sighed deeply. "I'm just tired of being misunderstood and feared. I want to help humans lose their fear of death and the first step is to give them freedom from being under the thumb of the other Mythics."

I turned to Medusa to see how she was taking all this information in. She just shrugged like she wasn't sure.

"Medusa, I can see why you wear that veil. Who was it that cursed you?" He asked with a genuine sounding voice, but there was something else in there. Like when a lawyer asks a question that he already knows the answer to.

"Athena did this, but I blame Poseidon just as much," said Medusa. She said it coldly and firmly, but then recoiled as if she had said something that she shouldn't have.

"That sounds like the actions of those supposedly above-the-law Mythics. You have nothing to fear here, Medusa. I'd be just fine with you and your friend here starting with those two. They are some of the biggest blights that the humans face." Hades turned back to me and raised an eyebrow. "So, what do you say? Do you both want to be heroes and help me in saving humanity?"

I looked over to Medusa and saw that she was smiling. She nodded at me.

"We'd love to," I said.

"Excellent," he said as he leaned back and pressed his fingertips together. "Let's enjoy the parade and we can talk some more after. I want you both to enjoy your time here."

We had just barely entered the city and the procession had slowed quite a bit. Athena and Hephaestus were hamming it up and waving at all the cheering masses. The road was being littered with rose petals and I realized that it was the two dozen individuals with the baskets that were tossing them out in front of the two Mythics. I couldn't help but laugh again.

"Are they always this extravagant?" I asked either of the other occupants in the carriage. They both answered in the affirmative in unison, then I saw Medusa give Hades a little smile. It was nice to see her becoming more comfortable around him. I believed what he had said and he did seem to be genuine.

The parade went all the way around the city, which at its slower rate took over an hour. Then, we entered an area that had been cordoned off that led to the very center of the city. There was a huge area set up with tables and a slightly elevated stage with two main large thrones that were decorated with the same pink and red streamers that were strewn about the rest of the city. The two snotty Mythics stepped up and sat in the thrones and every one else sat around them.

Hades and the two of us took a table over to the side of the stage that wasn't elevated. I thought this was a promising move as it told me indirectly that Hades didn't feel the need to sit above everyone else. Maybe he was being one hundred percent honest. It would make life a little easier to have a Mythic on my side.

As the seats packed in with townsfolk who were all dressed for the occasion, Aphrodite stood to address the crowd. Everyone went silent and I expected that her giving a speech of some sort was an annual part of the festival.

"My darlings, my devotees, and those simply swept up in the tides of love! Welcome to Cythara, where passion blooms like our beautiful flowers and desire dances like the waves upon our golden shores. The Theogamia Festival is a time of grand romance, of whispered promises and extravagant gestures. Yes, we honor the glorious union of Zeus and Hera, but let us not forget that this festival is also about you.

About your longing, your devotion, and, of course, your love. Indulge yourselves, for what is love if not lavish?" Aphrodite continued her speech, but Hades began having a quiet side conversation with me as she droned on, mostly trying to get people to buy this or that to prove their love.

"I haven't had to sit through one of these sales pitches for years. She acts like love is her ultimate concern, but this festival fills up her storehouse more than the whole rest of the year. I'm only here because Hephaestus invited me to be his honored guest after I asked him to forge a bident for me," said Hades quietly.

"What's a bident?" I asked.

"Have you heard of a trident?" He asked. He seemed slightly disappointed that I didn't know what a bident was.

"Yes, like a spear with three pointy bits," I said. He sighed, either at my description, or that I was familiar with a trident but not his preferred weapon.

"I bident is like that, but with only two pointy bits. Poseidon wields a trident, I prefer the bident, and Zeus has his precious lightning bolt weapon. I'll be headed back to my island once the first day of this festival is over and I can pick up my weapon. Hephaestus may be just another terrible Mythic, but he does make the best arms and armor," said Hades.

"What island are you headed to?" I asked. I was still half listening to Aphrodite talk about some new present to prove your love that honestly sounded completely useless.

"Are you serious?" Asked Hades. He paused for a moment, but then continued when I shrugged in ignorance. "My island is also called Hades. It has the gateway to the underworld, but also a huge gymnasium and amphitheater. I try to have fun events as much as possible in all those locations, albeit fewer fun things happen in the underworld."

"Do you get many visitors who aren't dead there?" I asked.

"Very funny and yes. I do get a great many visitors. It was the biggest slap in the face that I could think of for Zeus, who named the island as a joke against me. I make a decent amount of drachma from tourists and some say it's the happiest place on Neos Ellas. The fact that Zeus and Poseidon hate that humans come to my island for fun just makes me smile. I'd like you and Medusa to accompany me to Hades. It would be safer to talk there about how we deal with our shared problems," he said, motioning over to the two Mythics.

I focused back on Aphrodite who seemed to be wrapping up her speech.

"Thank you all for making it to the Theogamia Festival! Buy gifts, enjoy the food and festivities, and most importantly spread the love!" Aphrodite finished her speech and everyone in this central area cheered and clapped. Aphrodite sat back down and watched as the people began to leave. She had a sly smile on her face and I suspected that it was because she had just successfully fooled these people into buying things that they didn't need just to fuel her greed.

"I'm not planning on buying any of her stupid little gifts," I said so that only my table could hear.

"The Theogamia Festival can also be a time for friends to buy gifts for each other you know," said Medusa.

"I guess I could get you a little something." This came from the people-pleasing side of me that feared losing friends. She immediately laughed which put me at ease.

"I was only joking. I don't want to give Mythics any more money than I have to," said Medusa. She quickly looked over at the Mythic that was sitting at the table with us currently. "No offense."

Hades shrugged it off. "None taken. I'm not going to buy any of the little gifts either. Speaking of drachma, my invitation for you to join me in Hades won't cost you anything. You'd be my special guests with free travel, entrance, food, fun, and a nice place to sleep for as long as you'd like to stay," he said.

"That sounds pretty good to me," I said.

"Me too," said Medusa. "Thank you, Mr. Hades, sir."

"Just Hades is fine. I'm glad that I was able to make some new friends at this insipid festival," he said as he stood and excused himself. "I'm going to go try to pick up my weapon and then go back to Hephaestus's guest house until it's time to leave. Where are you two staying so I can come by and pick you up for our trip tomorrow?"

"We hadn't checked out any of the local inns yet," I said.

"They will all be packed by now I'm sure of it. Please come stay with me when you tire of the festival. I know I said 'guest house' but it's basically a guest palace. I don't even know how many rooms there are, but I know that they are available," said Hades.

"We'd love to and I'm sure we will be there sooner rather than later," I said. We gave Hades a friendly little bow as we left to begin our second walk-about.

We ended up walking around for a couple of hours. There were quite a few things to see and some festival games that were eerily similar to ones I'd seen at the county fair. I even managed to win Medusa a small stuffed animal playing a strength testing game. I felt a little bad as I broke the contraption and the prize was more to get me to leave and stop apologizing. My guess was that all of these games were owned by the local Mythics and operated by humans either by force or threat.

It was just past midday when we both decided to head back to Hade's guest palace. The palaces were easy to find and his was the only one with a shadowy, black carriage parked out front. We walked into the entryway and looked around at the lavish decor and furnishings. I'd never been in a house like this before.

"Welcome. Did you get sick of the festival already?" Asked Hades.

"I think we saw all that we needed to see," I said.

"It's kind of just making me sad to see all the happy couples and knowing that I'll never have that," said Medusa. Hades looked surprised.

"If you don't mind me asking, Medusa, why do you think that?" Asked Hades. There was a reassuring sincerity to his tone that surprised me for some reason.

"Are you joking? Who would sign up for this?" Asked Medusa.

"Who wouldn't?" He asked. "You're an amazingly strong woman who has overcome more adversity than most people have to even think about facing. Being the Mythic that controls the gates of the underworld makes me uniquely qualified to make character judgements about people and you are a good person."

Medusa wiped her eyes and I could tell that she was smiling. I was starting to like Hades more and more. "So, did you pick up your bident?"

"Not yet. I probably won't see Hephaestus until after the feast tonight. We can leave first thing in the morning. I've taken a room on the main floor here so you two can have any rooms you like upstairs," said Hades.

"Do you know if there are any monsters around here that I could fight before bed?" I asked. He laughed before understanding that I was completely serious.

"Not that I know of, but you could ask some of the house staff or guards. They might know of something," he said. Then, he laughed again and shook his head as he left the room.

"There are still quite a few hours until nightfall. I'm going to go talk to the guards. Do you feel comfortable staying around here?" I asked Medusa.

"Yes, between the library, the gardens, and the comfy beds, I think I'll survive for a few hours," she said playfully.

I turned and looked around for a guard. I found a maid who pointed me in the right direction. There was a guardhouse hidden behind the main palace that looked to be able to hold a couple dozen people.

I knocked on the door and a regular sized man who looked like he'd just woken up opened the door. His eyes panned up to meet mine with a mixture of fright and awe. He must've never seen a non-Mythic my size.

"Can I help you?" He asked meekly.

"I'm a guest of Hades and I'm looking for a fight," I said. It was then I knew that I should've chosen my words better as the man fainted.

Chapter 18

Good Goal

When the guard woke up the first thing he saw was me standing over him. He screamed in such a way that caught me off guard. I laughed, but then felt bad about it.

"Take it easy. I'm not going to hurt you. I meant I'm looking for a monster to fight," I said. The man crawled backward while still looking quite scared. "You're safe. I'm one of the good guys. My name is Mae."

"I'm called Chrysanthos. Please don't tell the other guards that I fainted. They'd never stop making fun of me," he said.

"I won't say a word about it," I said. The man relaxed after that as if his greatest fear was receding back into the further corners of his mind.

"Thank you," he said. Even more of the tension released in him as the realization set in that his life wasn't being threatened by a superhumanly strong, giant of a woman. "You want to fight a monster?"

"Yes, have there been any monsters around?" I asked.

"As a matter of fact, Aphrodite had just given orders to exterminate some flying rodents that have been sleeping in her storehouse with greater frequency. She called them the minyades. It hasn't been a huge priority as they haven't done any damage, but she is getting sick of the smell and her storehouse is going to be filling up pretty soon. You could probably take care of that problem pretty easily," he said.

"I can definitely take care of that. Thanks, Chrysanthos. Sorry for scaring you earlier," I said.

"Your best bet is to go around sundown if you want to catch them as they wake up and leave the storehouse," he said.

"Oh, so you're saying that the monsters are probably inside the storehouse now?" I asked.

"There's a good chance. They seem to sleep during the day and be active at night. Only authorized personnel and the Mythics themselves are allowed to enter the storehouses, so that's why I recommend fighting them when they leave. We wouldn't want the storehouse to get damaged after all," he said.

"No, we wouldn't want that." I smiled as he had given me an idea and I was up for some mischief. I feel like I haven't had some proper mischief for decades. "That sound like a good plan. Thanks again. I'm going to go make sure I have everything I need to fight them after they leave the storehouse in the morning." I winked at him, which just left him a little confused.

I wouldn't be waiting until morning and I didn't care if the storehouse was collateral damage. I thought about running my actual plan by Hades, but I didn't need permission and then he'd have plausible deniability. It was a win-win. I did want to do a quick detour over to the docks to let Captain Galen know that we wouldn't be heading back with him. I needed to wait for it to be closer to nightfall anyway. I caught Medusa on the way out. She was sitting in a garden and reading.

"I'm going to go let Captain Galen know that we won't be going with him. Also, I found out about some more monsters to fight on the island, but I have to wait until it's darker out, so I won't be back until late," I said.

"Tell the Captain that I hope he has a good trip home. Do you want me to come with you for the monster fight just in case you want things to get rocky?" She asked.

"First of all, I love the petrification pun. Second, I think it's actually better for you to stay away from this fight. I have an ulterior motive for the timing and location. I'll tell you all about it on the way to the island tomorrow," I said.

"Sounds good." She went back to her reading and I headed to the docks.

As I walked through the streets of Cythara the rage in me was building, but I couldn't quite put my finger on it. I got to the docks and found Captain Galen's ship, but he wasn't there. I still had some time to kill before nightfall and I remembered that I had another resource that I could tap. I sat down on the docks looking out toward the water and I called out for Noctua. She flew to me from behind me as if she came from the city and landed on a dock post next to me.

"It's good to see you, Noctua. Thank you for coming when I called. Were you in Cythara already?" I asked. The talking owl did the weird head tilt thing that owls do and just stared at me.

"Is that really the question you want to ask me?" Asked Noctua. She was right. I had a more troubling question.

"You're right. I really wanted to know if you had any insight into why I was getting so angry just walking through the streets," I said.

"Where do you think the anger is coming from?" Asked Noctua.

"I don't know. Nothing here is reminding me of my relationship with Felix," I said. Then, I paused and thought about what I just said.

"I think you just answered your own question," she said and then moved which made it seem like she was about to fly off again.

"Wait. I just thought of one other question I need to ask," I said. Noctua settled back down on the post and stared at me again as if waiting. "Could I beat a Mythic in a fight?"

"The Mythics are invincible, so you can't kill them. You could have an advantage based on the fact that you've invested heavily in your Melanc humor though. Not only are you already physically stronger than some of the Mythics, you have a lot of Energy Points. If a Mythic runs out of EP in a fight they would be knocked out for a period of time. The same goes for you, but you've been driven to continue leveling up and getting stronger. The Mythics' complacency and lack of growth could be their downfall," she said.

"Thank you, Noctua. I'll think about what we talked about while I wait for the captain," I said.

The helpful owl flew off and disappeared over the rooftops of Cythara.

The thing about being able to knock out a Mythic as long as I had more EP than them, or used mine more efficiently, was really encouraging. It made me want to keep leveling up and getting as much strength and energy as possible. I went back to the first question that had been bothering me. Why was I getting so angry while walking through Cythara? I'd said that nothing here reminded me of my relationship with my husband Felix, but only after the war. Before the war we would've fit in perfectly with all of these love-struck festival attendees.

Was I actually mad at Felix or was I mad at the war that changed him? Definitely him, I thought at first, but I wasn't confident. Just the fact that I was still thinking about him after I was dead was infuriating. Thankfully, a strong, calm voice stopped my train of thought in its tracks.

"Mae, it's good to see you. Are you already ready to leave?" Asked Captain Galen.

"Yes, I'm ready to leave, but I was actually coming to let you know that we weren't going to be needing a ride," I said. He looked a little disappointed at my unexpected announcement.

"Oh, that's too bad. I was really looking forward to having you on board. I think we all felt a little safer with you around. I understand though. You're an adventurous type and I figured you might want to go exploring. There's a lot to see out there. Do you mind me asking where you're headed?" He asked.

"Hades invited us to his island. I think we'll start there and then explore a bit more of the world," I said.

"I know you can take care of yourself, but be careful with that one. From what I hear, he usually has an agenda and I think he may not be above using others to get what he wants," he said, sounding like a concerned father or something. It seemed strange, but then I remembered that I wasn't a woman at an advanced age here. I probably was young enough to be his daughter and I knew that he was just being protective.

"I already know what his agenda is and he's asked me to help him with it outright. There didn't seem to be any subterfuge," I said.

"Do you mind me asking what his agenda is?" He asked.

"Let me ask you a question first. What do you think about the Mythics?" I asked.

"I try not to think about them at all. Besides the tributes us sailors have to pay to Poseidon, we don't have much to worry about," he answered.

"What if you didn't have anything to worry about, tributes-wise?" I asked. His face went from confused to relieved as he thought about the idea.

"I guess that would be pretty nice for everyone. Wait, is Hades trying to make it so no one has to pay tributes?" Asked the captain.

"Something like that. I thought it was a good goal, so I said I'd help him," I said.

"I have difficulty believing that a dozen Mythics would willingly agree to give up their tribute requirements," he said with a great deal of skepticism in his voice.

"Their will isn't going to have much say in the matter," I said with a smile.

He paused for a moment as if considering what to say next. "Just be careful, Mae. I may not like the Mythics too much, but I trust Hades even less. I'd hate for him to hurt you."

"I'm invincible, Captain Galen. He can't hurt me," I said.

"There are many ways to be hurt besides the physical, Mae. Just promise me that you'll keep an eye out for any tricks he may have up his sleeve," said the captain as he extended his hand out for a handshake of agreement.

I pulled him into a big hug and lifted him off the ground with ease. He patted me on the back as he was helpless to do anything else. Then, I sat him back down. "Sorry about that. I don't know why I did that."

"It's quite alright. I hope you have a good trip. You and Medusa were the best charter guests I've ever had," he said as he straightened out his ruffled uniform.

"I'll tell her and she said to tell you that she wishes you a safe trip home," I said. He bowed at me and jumped over to his ship. I wondered if I'd ever see him again. I thought back to the hug and why I'd done that. Captain Galen reminded me of my father, but only the best parts of him. He really did seem to care and I'd do my best to keep the promise.

I walked around the docks on the northern side of the island until the sun began to set. It was way more fun than walking around the city looking at the happy couples and I was able to see all sorts of boats from crusty fishing vessels to high-end sailing ships. I was excited about my next stop the whole time I was wandering. I headed to the west side of the island where Aphrodite's storehouse was located.

The streets had cleared out pretty well and I tried to make sure that no one saw me by the storehouse.

The building had columns across its facade and a statue of Aphrodite standing tall out front. The statue was about twenty to thirty feet tall. There were two guards by the entrance and I didn't want them to get hurt so I needed to figure out a way of getting them away from the building. The storehouse was enough away from the city that I had some room to work and it was dark enough that I shouldn't be able to be seen if I jumped high enough. My plan came together.

I was as far out in front of the storehouse as I could be where I could throw a decent sized stone and still be accurate. I activated Ballistos with all five EP added to maximize damage. I threw the semi-spherical stone overhead with both arms and then immediately squatted down, waited for Mighty Leap to be available and jumped higher than I'd ever jumped. I landed as close as I dare to the northern part of the clearing where it met up with the city. My hope was that it would look to the guards as if I'd just ran up from the city and not from where the stone came from.

The guards were on full alert when I ran up to them. I showed them that I didn't have a weapon in hand and gave them my best acting skills. "Was that a siege engine attack? It looked like it came from over there," I said, pointing more south of my throwing point just in case. They seemed to be on board. "You go find that machine and disable it and I'll go find more guards."

Maybe it was the fact that I was much larger and stronger than them or maybe they just believed me, but it worked. They ran off toward where I had pointed and I pretended to run toward the city. Once they were far enough out, I returned to examine the damage of my first attack on the Mythics. The statue of Aphrodite was struck around the shins and lay face down in the dirt. The rock had continued through and rolled to the front of the storehouse destroying one of the pillars.

Now the real fun could begin.

Chapter 19

THE STOREHOUSE

I sprinted toward the storehouse doors and activated Raging Bull. I put my fists out in front of me and they were the first point of contact with the heavy wooden doors. The doors didn't stand a chance. They burst into splinters and chunks clattered inside along with me. The inside of the storehouse reminded me of a modern warehouse. A couple rows of wooden shelves followed along the outside walls with about ten feet between them.

I didn't have time to take in all the treasures and knick-knacks that lined the shelves. I was too focused on the three humanoid bats that were flying at me from the rafters. I picked up a nearby chunk of wood from the door and threw it at the nearest attacker. The creature was able to dodge the attack, but I had managed to mess up its initial strike. The other two creatures were able to connect with clawed strikes that did nothing, except put slashes on my clothing.

The second monster stuck around for a follow-up attack and I was able to connect with a punch to its oddly feminine face. The punched creature crashed to the ground in front of me. It was only momentarily dazed. I quickly grabbed one of its wings and began to use it as a weapon. I smashed the weaponized bat into the third bat who had swung around for another attack. The bat that was struck flew into one of the sets of shelves causing everything in that section to fall to the ground.

I swung the still held bat around and let go in order to hurl it toward the shelves on the opposite side of the store house. It wasn't able to correct itself enough to halt the momentum and it crashed through another set of shelves.

I picked up a ten foot section of shelving and activated Raging Bull again toward the monster I'd just thrown. I became a ten foot wide battering ram and hit the still dazed monster and more shelving. I was trying to do as much damage as possible, not only to the bats, but also to the storehouse. My last attack took one of the bats out of the fight as another latched onto my back. This would be the last mistake this humanoid bat would make.

I squatted down as it continued scratching at my back. I was able to grab onto its wings which had been partially wrapped around me. It had no chance of escape. I activated Mighty Leap and smashed into the ceiling of the building with a crunch. A moment later, myself and the squished bat fell down to the floor along with a big chunk of the ceiling. Luckily, the ceiling fell into yet another section of shelving.

The last bat looked at me from across the room and then up at the new hole in the ceiling. I wasn't sure how they got in and out before, but it was clear that the monster's current plan was to fly out of that hole at full speed. I had to get the timing right to finish this. I could only imagine that the guards would be returning soon after all of the noise that I'd been making.

I activated Mighty Leap for the final time of this fight. My goal was to exit through the hole in the ceiling as the bat monster exited. I rocketed through the ceiling just as the bat attempted a similar maneuver. I grabbed onto the monster and continued my trajectory. I looked at my map which allowed me to freeze time and also see where I'd be landing.

I snapped back to real time, positioned the bat monster under my knees, and held it there until I landed. My landing zone was a ways south of the storehouse about halfway to the palaces. I landed bat first and the familiar gold coin floated above its body. I grabbed the hundred drachma coin immediately and ran as quietly as possible back to the guest palace. I guessed that the bat monsters were some sort of team as no coins had appeared when I defeated the others. I didn't worry about it too much as I didn't care that much about the drachma anyway.

I didn't see anyone as I slunk up the stairs and found an empty room. I couldn't stop smiling over how well I felt that went. It was my first strike against the Mythics and I wished I could see the look on Aphrodite's face when she saw the state of her precious storehouse. I laid down in the lavish bed and drifted off to sleep.

I had another nightmare about Felix while I slept. This one was not as intense of a situation as the last one, but the emotional response was just as strong. It was a time when Felix's anger came through after another episode where he felt like he was being attacked. He ended up breaking one of the few gifts that I'd received from a friend. It was a picture frame with a quote in it. It was something that she thought would help me get through the tough times.

I still remembered the quote. Felix read it before he yelled at me, grabbed the frame, and threw it on the ground. It said, "Make the best use of what's in your power and take the rest as it happens." It wasn't meant to be an attack, but I think it hit a nerve as most of what happened to me was out of my control and in his. I woke up as the glass in the frame shattered on the ground. The feeling of impotent helplessness filled me, but it shifted to anger as I processed it further.

Was this how Aphrodite would feel about her storehouse attack? Impotent helplessness? I kind of hoped so. I realized that I wasn't alone.

"Good morning," said a familiar voice. Hades was sitting across the room smiling in my direction. "Are you okay?"

"I'm fine. I just didn't expect to hear you right as I woke up," I said.

"Bad dream?" He asked.

"Something like that," I answered.

"We should probably try to depart as soon as possible this morning. Judging from the state of your clothing, you already know about the exciting news from last night," said Hades.

"Tell me what you know and I'll fill in the blanks," I said. I moved to sitting on the edge of the bed closest to Hades.

"My sources tell me that the storehouse of Aphrodite was attacked last night. I've heard everything from monstrous bats to rocks thrown from siege engines. What was your involvement?" He asked.

"There weren't any siege engines, just a very strong woman. There were large bat monsters, but I defeated them. Most of that fight was inside the storehouse and there may have been some damage," I said. I couldn't contain my smile, but he didn't reciprocate.

"The guards didn't see you during the attack?" He asked.

"I don't think so. I was pretty careful and my plan went about as well as I could've hoped," I said.

"I'm perfectly fine with the outcome, my only worry would be that the other Mythics figure out our plan before we have a chance to implement it. The element of surprise may be our best bet, but I'll trust you in saying that you don't think you were seen," said Hades.

"I'm ready to leave when you are," I said.

"Gather your friend and meet me at the carriage. We must move quickly while there is still confusion about the attacks," said Hades. I nodded and headed out to find Medusa. I had to check four rooms before I was able to find her. I let her know that Hades was looking to leave as soon as possible and she had no issues. We were at the carriage within minutes since we didn't really have much except for what we could easily carry on our backs.

We rode north through the city and took the shortest route to the docks. Hades's vessel was on theme for him. It was a large, black ship with black sails. We boarded and instantly saw the sailors moving about at a hurried pace trying to make the ship ready to sail. Another carriage pulled up beside the ship and Hephaestus got out and stared up at us.

"Relax. He's just delivering my weapon. I sent a messenger to tell him to bring it here and that it was urgent," said Hades. I guess I had looked a little worried that I had messed things up. Hades walked to the gangway to greet Hephaestus.

Hephaestus walked up the gangway and stood on the main deck. Two humans followed him up to the deck. They came over to Hades and presented the large bident that they had carried between them. Hades picked it up and immediately focused shadowy energy through it. It looked absolutely terrifying.

"Who's your large friend?" Asked Hephaestus unbothered by the shadow manipulation. "I saw you both at the same table, but I didn't get a chance to come over and introduce myself."

"This is Mae. She's helped out quite a few towns by defeating nearby monsters for them. She's a heroic adventurer and I've asked her to accompany me to help with a few monsters around my island," said Hades.

"Nice to meet you, Mae. Monsters, huh? Did you hear about the monsters that were recently defeated over at Aphrodite's storehouse?" Asked Hephaestus.

"Hades told me about it this morning," I said. I wasn't lying, but I was being guarded with the information for obvious reasons.

"The storehouse guards said that a woman who fits your description was at the storehouse. The timing seems suspect and your clothes do look a little worse for wear," said Hephaestus. I felt like I was being interrogated by a policeman for a second. This was before I remembered that I didn't care about the other Mythics or their opinions.

"It must've been a scary time for those guards. I'm glad none of them got hurt. There's probably a lot of confusion about what they saw there. What I can tell you is that I slept comfortably in the guest palace and my clothes get pretty torn up on a regular basis. I'm sure Hades can vouch for me," I said.

"I sure can. Mae would've been at the guest palace when the attacks took place if I understand the timing of everything correctly," said Hades.

"Well, as much as I trust your word, Hades, I'd like to ask Mae to accompany me to talk to the guards. I'm sure they can confirm that Mae wasn't the person they spoke with at the storehouse and she'd be fully cleared," he said.

"That won't be necessary or possible. I need to be heading back to my island and Mae is my guest," said Hades. He was obviously a tad perturbed at Hephaestus' lack of respect for him or his word.

"Come with me," said Hephaestus. He pulled out a sword and pointed it at me then motioned it toward the gangway. I didn't mean to laugh in his face, but I did. He didn't like it.

"No, I don't think I will," I said. "You heard Hades. I'm his guest and he told you where I was."

Hephaestus didn't like my answer or complete lack of respect toward him. He responded to it by bringing the sword closer to me. I grabbed the blade with both hands and attempted to yank it out of his hands. It didn't budge, but neither did either of our grips. I used this against him. I shifted my weight and swung him around with all my strength. He rolled down the gangway and back onto the docks. The look on his face was priceless.

Hades yelled some nautical terms and the gangway was quickly retracted while the ship pulled away from the docks. I stood by the railing and watched as Hephaestus got up and put his sword away. He was fuming.

"Thank you for the weapon, Hephaestus. No hard feelings," yelled Hades. It was so perfect and Hephaestus's face was beet red by this point. When we were far enough away from the docks, all three of us cracked up laughing. I had begun my war on Mythics and I was having fun in the process.

The ship gained speed as the sails filled and we headed west on the Naxion Sea. According to my partially filled in map, we would need to travel straight west and then a little north to make it to the island of Hades. I was excited to finally get all the details about how we would be dealing with the Mythics, but I knew that it would require patience. We had to make these changes systematically or there was a fear that all the Mythics might have the chance to regroup and fight me all together.

I was invincible, but I wasn't stupid.

"Let's just focus on enjoying the sea air and taking in the beautiful seascape until we see my island. That's when we get serious. Well, actually you should enjoy some good food and entertainment and then we'll get serious." Hades walked away still smiling. I could understand why he'd be a bit gloomy most of the time, but it was nice to be able to help someone find a little happiness. Even though he was a Mythic, he was the most hated and despised of them and that endeared me to him in a weird way. I almost felt a little sorry for him.

The day passed uneventfully. Medusa and I slept in a much nicer room below deck than Captain Galen had been able to offer. Nothing against the man, but he couldn't compete with this experience. The vision I had as I slept was stranger this time or at least it felt that way.

I was in the bathroom staring down toward the sink. I was looking at the gathered, broken pieces of the picture frame gift from my friend. I was trying to piece it back together when a shard of glass that I hadn't seen was still attached to the frame cut into my finger. I dropped the pieces into the sink and started running the cut under the tap. I looked up and realized that I was seeing this from my husband's perspective again. I hadn't seen any remorse or heard an apology, but the look on his face was full of regret and shame.

"Why? Why am I like this? Why do I do these things?" I cried and asked myself in the mirror, but it wasn't me. It was Felix. I had to just watch it all play out, no matter how much I wanted to leave this memory of his. I heard him whisper one last thing before I woke up. "Why is my brain broken?"

I don't know if these were meant to make me feel sorry for the man, but it was doing the opposite. I opened my eyes to the early morning light peaking into the room and just lay there processing his memory.

If he thought his brain was broken, why didn't he find help? Why did he continue hurting the people that loved him the most? He couldn't found help, processed his trauma, and had a life with us. The rage grew in me. The answer was so clear in my mind. I realized that I wasn't just angry at him. I was angry at myself. Why didn't I leave? As I thought about it, the dissonance between my current situation and that one grew. I wasn't like during my life. I thought of how easily I had flipped Hephaestus around. I couldn't have done the same to Felix.

The fear and uncertainty came flooding back and I started feeling that vague unease that I had felt so many times during my marriage. It was a hopelessness that I hated myself for feeling or accepting, but I could only now understand why. Compared to the hope I had now and the power I felt, I was so weak and helpless. No, I was a survivor. I did what I could with the strength and will I had, which was nothing to what I had now.

My mind teetered back and forth like two sides of a debate winding down their rebuttals. In the end, the side that viewed the power I currently held as my main hope of surviving this world won. I didn't have power when I was alive, but I was different now. I showed my husband grace out of fear. Not just of him, but of the unknown.

There would be no grace here. The Mythics were going to be defeated and I would never have to be a survivor again. I was now a freedom fighter with people counting on me. To put it in Hades's words, I was now a hero.

Chapter 20

HADES'S PALACE

We arrived on the island of Hades in the late afternoon of the next day. The most impressive part of our approach was the giant marble statue of Hades himself. It was difficult to tell how tall it was, but my guess would've been about a hundred feet tall. As we docked, Hades came over to me and began to give me all the information I would need for the rest of the day.

"I've sent messengers to all of the attractions around the island. Every vendor will know that you are my special guest shortly. You and Medusa will be able to eat anywhere you'd like and enjoy any of the shows or events without having to worry about drachma. My palace is on the north side of the island. All I ask is that you retire there for the evening so that I can share more of my plans with you. The people who work here and in my house are loyal to me as if their lives depend on it, so you are safe here," said Hades. Then, he departed his ship and disappeared into the shadows between two buildings.

I was excited at the prospect of having fun at an amusement park of sorts since I'd never gotten the opportunity, but I was also excited to get on with the plan. Medusa placing her hand on my arm snapped me out of my thoughts.

"Are you okay? What did Hades say?" Medusa asked. I relayed all of the information to her that I'd just received and her face lit up.

"What are you so happy about?" I asked.

"We get to enjoy the happiest place on Neos Ellas for free as VIP guests and you're not excited?" She said rhetorically. "Why are we even still standing here? Let's explore!"

We ran off of the boat and into the theme park. The engineering of the place was incredible. There were rides that used pulleys and gears to move carts around and others that used rushing water for forward motion. There was nothing that a modern person on Earth would call a roller coaster, but it was impressive. We wanted to try all of them. It didn't seem like the rides had been made for people as large as myself, but surprisingly, each ride had a variant seating arrangement that could accommodate a larger rider.

"These must be designed so that even the Mythics can enjoy them," I said, mostly to myself as I processed the information.

"Of course they are. Why would Hades make rides that he can't enjoy?" Her words made a lot of sense and didn't require a response. She continued going from place to place with a huge grin that I could see through her bee-keeper's hat. Her joy was infectious and soon we were both acting like little kids at Disneyland. For the next few hours, all of our past concerns and troubles didn't exist. We crammed as much fun as possible into the day and only began looking for food options as the sun set.

The most high-end food option was simply called 'Ambrosia'. We sat down at a table and a waitress came over to us in less than a minute.

"Welcome to Ambrosia, honored guests," she began with a bow and handed us both menus. "Please, order whatever you'd like and I'll bring it out to you as soon as possible."

I didn't know what a lot of the food options were since there weren't any pictures and the Greek food names were not something I'd come across before. I shrugged at Medusa and she took the hint.

"Could you ask the chef to cook up a couple of his favorites or specialties along with whatever you recommend for drinks?" Asked Medusa.

"Absolutely," she said taking the menus back and hurrying off toward the kitchen. She returned a moment later with deep red, non-fermented grape juice and a cup of water for each of us. The flavor of the grape juice was incredible.

We sat and sipped on our beverages while talking about our favorite rides and it wasn't long before the food began to arrive. The tables were about six feet across and round. We sat toward one side and the whole other side was full of serving dishes of various shapes and sizes. The meal consisted of a couple of well-prepared and presented fish fillets, fruits, and vegetables. We ate to our heart's content and were able to tackle most of the offering. I had eaten two or three times what Medusa ate, but she didn't make me feel bad about it as she was also stuffed by the end of the meal.

"Are you ready to head over to Hades's palace?" I asked.

"Yes, but you may have to cart me over there," she said as she patted her stomach.

The waitress came over and continued with the great service. "Would the honored guests like a carriage to be called?"

"Yes, please," I said with a smile. "And please thank the chef for the wonderful meal." The waitress bowed and hurried off again. After another period of chatting and digesting, a carriage pulled up to the front of the restaurant and the waitress let us know that it was ready. I thanked her again and we walked to the carriage.

"Where would the honored guests like to go?" The driver asked as he politely helped us onto the carriage.

"Hades's palace, please," said Medusa. She was still struggling with her food baby and looked to be getting sleepy as well. It made sense as we'd been hurriedly walking for hours before stopping for the massive meal. The driver bowed, climbed up to his seat, and then encouraged the two horses toward our destination. It wasn't long before we arrived.

The palace was a tall, gloomy building. Dark gray stones and blackened wood made up the facade. There were overhangs and gargoyle-esque stone outcroppings spaced evenly about the front. The shadows from the flickering torchlight danced around the palace unnaturally or at least it seemed unnatural. As we approached, I realized that it was the strange angles that gave the palace this otherworldly feel.

Hades greeted us just inside the main entrance hall. "Welcome to my humble abode. I hope you were able to have fun for the last few hours," he said. The interior was dimly lit and the dancing shadows played similar tricks on the inside of the building. Hades looked at Medusa who looked as tired as can be. "Thanatos can show you to your rooms. I might suggest that Medusa get some sleep while Mae and I have a discussion in my study."

The mystery of who Thanatos was didn't last long as he soon appeared in the shadows of a doorway nearby and bowed low. He reminded me of the butler in the original Addams Family show. He was tall and gaunt.

"I'm fine with that plan," I said. Medusa nodded thankfully. She looked so tired at this point and I could always fill her in on the details in the morning.

Thanatos took us to our rooms and then brought me to the study where Hades was sitting by a large fireplace in a massive leather chair. He directed me to sit in a matching chair across from him.

"Mae, I'm going to get straight to business. I have a prison that is capable of holding the Mythics, but it must be cleared out as it is nearing capacity. My second issue is that I don't believe you are strong enough to defeat all of the Mythics yet. The first problem may be our solution to the second. If you enter Tartarus and defeat the titans within, you could grow strong enough to defeat the Mythics. The key to Tartarus is this golden band," he said as he held up a gold ring. My first thought was that there was no way it would fit me.

"It's a tad small," I said.

"It's not bound to a specific size. When you equip the object, it will conform to the finger it is on. Not only that, it will also only be removable by your will," he paused briefly. "There's one other way for the key to leave you, but you don't need to worry about that."

This immediately sparked my curiosity. "What's the other way to remove it?"

"If the wearer's finger, hand, or arm is severed from the rest of the body then the key can be removed. You don't have to worry about that, do you?" He asked.

"I guess I don't. So once the Key of Tartarus is equipped, in my case, it can only be removed by my will?" I asked.

"That is correct," said Hades. "You are uniquely qualified to be trusted with this key."

"How does it work?" I asked.

"Put it on and I'll show you," he said. I did as he asked and the gold band grew in size and then tightened around my right ring finger. It wasn't uncomfortable, I could hardly feel it there. "If you point the key forward and will the portal to Tartarus to open, it will appear before you. The portal will open and close at your whim and you are able to enter and leave whenever you'd like, but no other entities can enter or leave without your permission. It's the perfect prison, but it can only contain so much power. That is why the titans must be destroyed to make room."

I extended my right hand and willed the portal to open. A swirling oval opened in front of me growing from fist-sized to about ten feet tall in about a second. I began to walk into to portal. Hades said one last thing before I entered. "May I enter Tartarus with you?"

I answered in the affirmative and we both walked through the portal. Tartarus was so different than any place I'd ever seen and it took me a moment to take everything in. The ground was the color of a terracotta pot. The rust orange contrasted the inky darkness above. There were no stars in the sky, but there was no ceiling that I could see either. I couldn't see any specific light source, but I could see well enough. It was the same amount of light that you might have early in morning just before dawn.

"Where are these titans?" I asked, worried about us getting attacked at any moment.

"Tartarus is vast. Unless you will the portal to open near a certain prisoner, it will open to a random barren area. This is great for when dropping off new prisoners and for times when you just want a moment alone. The latter is what I'll miss the most. I do ask that you return the key to me when your task is complete," said Hades.

"I have no problem with that. I don't see a need for the key once I have the other Mythics locked away. That's assuming that you wouldn't want to release them," I said.

"We both have the same goal. It may be time to leave this place," he said. That's when I felt the ground beginning to quake. "May I leave Tartarus with you?"

"I looked around, but didn't yet see what was making the ground shake. Yes, let's leave for now," I said. We both stepped back through the portal and were once again in Hades's study. "What was that?"

"That was one of the titans. Sometimes they get lucky and come across one of my portals, but even they can't exit without the keymaster's permission," said Hades as he sat back down in the nice leather chair. I dismissed the portal and sat down across from him again.

"If a titan is able to make the ground quake, how do you expect me to defeat something that large?" I asked.

"They all have their weaknesses and they are far from unbeatable. Zeus has defeated them every time one becomes a threat. They seem to be tied to the elements, but no one truly knows their origins. We do know that at their core is a crystal and if one is able to remove the crystal from them, they dissipate. If the crystal isn't destroyed, the titans reform and grow over time. Zeus didn't want to destroy the titans, only to stop them. He had me cast their crystals into Tartarus for safe keeping. Now his weakness in failing to destroy them will be your strength," said Hades.

"When you say the titans are tied to the elements, what do you mean exactly?" I asked.

"Fire, wind, water, and earth are the elements. You'll have to see them to understand and I know that you can find their weaknesses once you see them. If Zeus can figure it out, certainly you can." He rose from the chair and began walking out of the room. He stopped before he left fully and turned back toward me. "You can have as much time as you need to defeat the titans and grow in strength, but I'd caution you to work quickly. Aphrodite won't be happy about her storehouse being destroyed and Hephaestus seemed to know that you had something to do with the attack. It won't be long before the Mythics come looking for you and the element of surprise may be your greatest weapon. I had Thanatos set a gift on your bed. If you're going to be a hero, you might as well look the part."

I nodded and he continued out of the room. I would get some sleep, talk to Medusa in the morning, and then get started on dealing with the titans. First, I ran up the stairs to see what my present was. I felt like a little kid again.

There was a large piece of fabric laid out on the bed. It was pearlescent white with golden hems. I took off my tattered clothing that I was a little embarrassed about now that I could see the state of it. When I equipped it, I felt a rush of power and the embarrassment melted away. The new tunic draped over and around me with a gold rope functioning as a belt and I made it look good. I wasn't sure what the rush of power was, but a quick glance at my status confirmed the changes.

I read through the information with my mouth refusing to close at the awe of it all. This was an incredible gift.

Mae June Cohen

Level 4 - Kolossos

HP - 230/230

EP - 500/500

---

15   Sanguin: This humor has a direct correlation to constitution and HP.

17   Coleric: This humor has a direct correlation to speed and agility.

15   Flegmat: This humor has a direct correlation to intellect and luck.

42   Melanc: This humor has a direct correlation to strength and EP.

This had to do with my newly equipped tunic. That was the only explanation that made sense, but I wanted more information. As if my will made the new tab appear, a section called 'Equipment' appeared in my menus. I guess I hadn't really had a reason to look before since I hadn't really equipped anything special, so it made sense to show it now. In the equipment tab there was a list of everything that I was currently wearing.

Tartarus Key Ring

A simple golden band that allows the wearer to open a portal to enter and exit Tartarus. Only the wearer can decide who can utilize the portal.

Arachne's Tunic of Power

The most perfectly woven garment ever created. It was created by Arachne herself during a challenge against the Mythic, Athena. Arachne won the contest and the tunic was imbued with power. Wearing this tunic grants +10 to all humors. It is impervious to all damage.

I snapped back out of my menus and stared down at the tunic in awe. I'd read the story of Arachne in Ancient Greek mythology. She'd been turned into a spider for her victory. This was the perfect thing for me to wear as my previous clothing had been shredded multiple times. I guess I didn't have to worry about that anymore. I was excited to see how much stronger it had made me. I did look rather heroic as well, which was a bonus. The equivalent of two full levels of Melanc, ten points, had been added. I wondered if Hades was a hugger, but decided he'd probably just like a simple 'thank you' more.

Chapter 21

THE TITANS

My nightmarish vision as I slept ended up being of one of the many times Felix woke up in a cold sweat while producing guttural yells. This particular time was when we had moved into a smaller apartment after our son, David, had moved out. I remember meeting a concerned neighbor at the door.

"Mae, is everything all right?" Asked the man who lived in the apartment above us. His wife waited above us on the stairs leading back up to their unit. The look on her face was more of a disgusted, frustration which was a stark contrast to her husband's look of concern and care. He worked at a local church so it was par for the course to try and care for others in his case. I can't blame his wife. I'm sure she had seen the occasional bruise on me as we passed at the main entrance. I knew she hated Felix and I didn't hold it against her.

"He just had a nightmare again. I'm so sorry that it woke you," I said. Felix was out of bed and standing just out of view behind the open front door. His expression was blank. I hated when I couldn't tell what was going on in his head. Walking on eggshells was more mentally tiring when they were invisible in the first place. I never knew when a comment would set him off.

"Do either of you need anything?" He asked. He was a genuinely good man who cared deeply for people. Felix used to be like him. Then the war taught him that people you care for die harder than people you don't. That was what I was beginning to understand about him.

"No, Jimmy. We're fine. He'll be back to sleep soon enough," I said.

"You can stay with us whenever you'd like, Mae. If you ever need a safe space," said Jimmy. His wife took a step down the stairs, but it seemed unintentional. It was like she wanted to gently elbow her husband, but wasn't close enough. He had said something that he shouldn't have, but he didn't know that Felix could hear him.

In a flash, Felix swung the door open and punched the man square in the nose. The look on his face was so troubling, like a snarling animal. I'd seen a hint of this face at times, but never this unfiltered. The man fell to the floor holding a nose that was most likely broken. His wife was down the stairs in a flash providing as good of first aid as she could with a now red handkerchief. Felix cocked back to throw another punch, possibly at the man's wife as she had approached quickly and Felix didn't do well with threatening situations.

I held his arm back at the elbow and was able to arrest the forward momentum. The force of the movement transferred to me and I landed on the ground next to the punched man. Jimmy helped me up and I positioned myself between Felix and the now fearful couple. Felix retreated back into apartment without a word while I handled the apologies.

Jimmy and his wife refused to call in the assault for my sake, but they did advise me to seek help. They never came to the door again, but I don't remember us living there for much longer either. Felix burned all the bridges everywhere we lived. This fact left me as an inaccessible island. It wasn't until he died that I was really able to have good friends again. When Felix died, he took a good amount of my fear and shame with him.

I woke up to Medusa shaking my shoulder gently.

"Mae, wake up. You're having another nightmare," she said, backing off slightly as I sat up in the comfortable bed. I woke up in a bad mood. Why did I stay? Why didn't I take Jimmy's advice and seek help?

"It was just another flashback of my terrible husband and my terrible previous life," I said sadly. Medusa knew my story by now. She knew that I had endured so much with this man.

"Can I ask you a question about your life before Neos Ellas?" Asked Medusa. She came over and sat toward the foot of the bed.

"Of course. You're my closest friend," I said. Medusa had probably become the closest friend I'd ever had.

"Why did you put up with him?" She asked solemnly. I could tell that her heart hurt a bit, just by asking the question.

"I don't know if I can explain it in a way that makes sense. Looking back, I don't understand why or how I stayed as long as I did. It's like I wasn't even making choices. I thought I was, but I wasn't. I had this idea in my head that leaving wasn't an option. Like when you're in a dream, and you try to run, but your legs don't work. That's how it felt. Every time I thought about leaving, I'd hear this voice in my head asking these terrifying questions. 'Where would you go? Who would take you in? How would you survive on your own?' So I did nothing. At some point, I just accepted that my life was what it was. You stop hoping for change because it's easier to survive when you don't expect better. It's like being stuck in deep water, too tired to swim, so you just let yourself float. I told myself all kinds of things to make it make sense. And the worst part? I wasn't even thinking those thoughts on purpose. They were just there. Like breathing. Like blinking. Now that he's gone, I wonder how much of my life I actually lived. How much of it I was just existing. I wish I could go back and shake myself awake, but I know I wouldn't have listened," I said.

"That's terrible. I can't imagine what I'd have done in your situation," she said.

"I know what you'd have done," I responded. She looked confused at the response. I smiled at the thought, I couldn't help myself. "You would've petrified him anytime he acted up. It's a real gift you have there."

Medusa smiled, but there was some sadness there too. "I wish I could've saved you some of that pain."

"Helping me heal from it is the next best thing," I said, as I stood up to my full height and shook off the soft blanket that had surrounded me. It was Medusa's first time seeing the tunic, but there was another reason for her look of surprise.

"Are you taller again?" She asked incredulously.

"Only a little bit. The tunic gives me some extra power. When I grow in power, I get a bit taller. I guess the extra muscle has to have a larger frame to attach to. I have to stop growing at some point though. Or I won't be able to fit through doors," I said. I was glad to be on a different topic and even more excited to test my new strength.

I told her everything that I'd learned about Tartarus, the titans, and the tunic. She was on board with a prison for the Mythics, but worried about the titans I'd have to defeat.

"Do you want me to come with you?" She asked.

"No. I'm not sure if your powers would even work on the titans. Plus, I'd just be worrying about you the whole time. I'll probably just be hopping back and forth between Tartarus and here after each fight though, so it's not like I'll be gone for too long," I said. This was a bit of a stretch as I had no idea how well I'd do fighting the titans or how long a fight with one would take even.

She nodded her head in agreement and it was time. I was not frightened at all to fight these titans, which I knew came from how I'd come to trust my invincibility. Even if it was a war of attrition, I'd beat them eventually. That's what I kept telling myself anyway. Decades of frailty has a way of conditioning your mind to fear all sorts of things. Uneven ground could have caused a fall that would've broken multiple bones and could have taken years for me to come back from. Now, I'm going to fight monsters that could destroy whole cities.

I thought about the Tartarus portal opening near an air element titan and the portal appeared in front of us. As I stepped through, I heard one last thing from Medusa.

"Good luck."

I clenched my fists and stepped through the portal. I closed it behind me and shielded my eyes from the gusting wind swirling around me. I noticed that I had to lean forward, into the wind, to keep my balance. I decided to try to get out of the wind for a second and get a bird's eye view. Maybe I'd be able to see where the titan was. This was a mistake.

As I squatted down, I was barely able to stay upright. I activated Mighty Leap after the prerequisite three seconds. I tried to jump straight up, but the wind gusted and I found myself flying backward with no control whatsoever. I hit the ground at a weird angle and did my best impersonation of a tumble weed with each new gust of wind rolling me further.

When the winds died down, a form began to solidify a few hundred feet from me. It was easily four times my size and it was laughing at me. I got up, admittedly a little heated, and sprinted toward the air titan, I activated Raging Bull and attempted to bash into the figure. It wasn't as solid as I'd hoped and I ran right through it as it dissipated back into the gusting wind. How do you destroy the wind? I looked around as I tried to find a solution to this puzzle.

There were some odd-looking trees in the distance and some rocks and boulders here and there. These would be my weapons. Remembering the forest where I met Medusa, I switched targets and hurled a fairly large rock toward the closest tree. I had put a few EP into the throw to ensure the tree would take enough damage to fit into the next part of my idea. The stone struck and the tree fell toward me.

I ran over to the fallen tree and picked it up. I intended to use it as a comically large baseball bat, which it resembled at this point. I swung it around from a point near what was the top of the tree, but the force of my swing broke the part I was holding off. I had to move a little further down and grip the tree with both hands in order to swing it without it breaking. I swung the implement around in a large circular motion and just kept it going. Once I was spinning, it was fairly easy to keep it going and the wind didn't seem to have as much of an effect on me. Either that, or the wind I was making was disrupting the titan's control.

I just kept spinning around while moving in the direction of the titan. Eventually, the tree was sweeping right through the monster and at one point, I heard a loud pop and the winds died down completely. I slowed and came to rest. I dropped the tree on the ground and looked around for the air titan, but nothing solidified. I caught a glint out of the corner of my eye and saw the familiar gold coin floating a few feet off the ground. I ran over to grab the coin and noticed that it was floating directly over a shard of clear crystal. Looking around, I found a few more shards. The fragments seemed to form a pattern from a point of impact close to where the wind titan had been solidifying.

Breaking this crystal must be the way to defeat them. I just need to find each titan's crystal and destroy it. That's how I win this. I felt the ground beginning to shake again, much like it had when I'd visited Tartarus before with Hades. I was a hundred drachma richer and one titan's worth of experience stronger.

"That wasn't too tough," I said out loud to myself reassuringly. The quaking became stronger and I saw a line of dirt that was being pushed up. Like when a cartoon character was tunneling underground, except much larger. I wasn't sure what to expect, but it wasn't stacks of boulders. That's what came out of the ground. Hundreds of large stones, swirling around each other, in a fluid motion that didn't seem possible. They ranged in size from basketball to sedan and all coalesced into a form similar to the air titan. This was no doubt an earth titan.

I picked up my tree weapon and attempted to bludgeon the rocky titan. I wasn't sure why I thought the tree was stronger than stone, but I was quickly shown the error of my ways. The tree cracked loudly against the boulders and vibrated down to my arms. I let go and allowed it to drop to the ground. My thought was that somewhere inside the earth titan there had to be a similar crystal. I just needed to find it. The earth titan retaliated by swinging one of its massive arms toward me. I was able to dive to the side before the boulders that made up its arm made a dent in the ground where I'd just been standing.

It swung another arm around, but the extra speed that I had now because of the tunic was sufficient to allow me to dodge again. The titan didn't move overly fast, so I was able to time my dodges well enough. After a few more strikes with me on the defensive, I decided to switch it up. I picked up the tree weapon again and executed a Mighty Leap with all my strength. My target was the head of the earth titan which I figured as a good spot to hide a crystal.

I reached the apex of my leap and then positioned the tree to strike first. The earth titan took the blow and crumbled into its component parts. The crystal was there among the rubble, but it quickly had boulders swirling around it as the earth titan reformed. I grabbed two fist sized stones and slammed them together with the crystal between them. The crystal shattered and the boulders and smaller rocks fell to the ground lifeless. I quickly grabbed the gold coin thinking I was already halfway to having an empty prison.

That's when the wind began to gust again. I thought that maybe the crystal had reformed from the air titan, but with a quick glance in that direction, I saw the broken crystal from the first monster. That meant that there wasn't just one of each like I had understood. How many could there be? I pondered as the new air titan began to form. At least I had more knowledge now and more projectiles.

I ran over to the pile of stones and boulders that made up the fallen earth titan and began throwing stone after stone at the new enemy's center. I kept putting only one EP into the activated Ballistos skill so I could just keep going until I got lucky. The projectiles were moving fast enough that they interrupted the majority of the wind that the titan was trying to pick up, but none of them were striking home.

Out of a mixture of annoyance and rage, I picked up the largest boulder that I could out of the pile and added all five points to it. This much larger projectile that I'd had to thrown with both arms was large enough to cover a large swath of the titan's center. It was enough to strike the crystal and the air titan dispersed. I picked up yet another gold coin and looked around. I didn't see anything so I opened the exit portal and walked through. Medusa was sitting down reading a book and glanced up at me as I closed the portal and almost immediately reopened another with another target in mind.

"How's it going?" She asked, her eyes going back to her reading.

"Great. I'm destroying titans and getting rich in the process," I said as I gave a little wave and stepped into the new portal to Tartarus.

"That's nice," said Medusa as the portal closed.

Chapter 22

THE EDGE

I had thought about a fire titan as I opened the new portal and came out close to a large mound of magma. I let the portal close and walked over to the mound. I poked my finger into the magma as a test. I knew it wouldn't hurt, but I was still curious. The mound began to jiggle like the world's most dangerous Jell-O as the glob grew taller. I grabbed at the magma with my full hand and pulled a molten chunk out of it. I tossed the quickly cooling molten rock behind me and it hit the ground with a sizzle. It quickly lost it's reddish glow and settled on dark gray.

The titan was slow. It was like fighting molasses. It had a few basic attacks, but they were easily dodged. Sometimes it would expel chucks of itself at me, which I would throw back with force until I noticed that it just reabsorbed the projectiles. It was clear that its main threat was the damage the heat could do to buildings, foliage, and people. It didn't bother me at all though. I could easily tear out chunks of the monster and toss them far enough away to make re-absorbing them a losing position. The titan lost more and more mass until it was finally small enough for me to just root around in it until I found its crystal. Once the crystal was destroyed, the mass cooled. I grabbed another gold coin.

I waited a moment, but no additional titans presented themselves. So far, I'd been fairly underwhelmed and was starting to feel pretty confident about going up against the Mythics. These titans weren't overly intelligent though and used obvious attack patterns. I didn't suppose that the Mythics would be the same.

My next target was a water titan which ended up being the easiest of all since I couldn't drown. It was a little humorous to me that the titan thought the fight was over as I swam around inside of it trying to get ahold of its crystal. When the crystal broke, I splashed to the ground harmlessly.

Now that I knew how to defeat each type of titan, I went into training mode. I used my skills as much as possible in the fights. I was able to move from Metrios to Empeiros, which was the next rank up, in Mighty Leap, Raging Bull, and Ballistos. This upgrade doubled their damage bonuses. I also unlocked a new skill called Thunderous Clap, but it only advanced to the Metrios level. Thunderous Clap was the move that I usually used to destroy the crystals and could be activated either barehanded or while holding objects such as stones.

Most importantly, I was able to advance to level five and I put all five points into my Melanc humor for more added strength.

After returning to Hades palace for the final time that evening, I lay in my bed and looked through all the ways that I had grown. I still had some work to do in Tartarus, but I was feeling pretty good about myself. My EP had only gotten into the low hundreds at any point, as I just kept coming back and allowing them to refill between fights. I was sure that I would be fine if my EP did run out, but the feeling of not being in control for a time was uncomfortable. I checked my stats again while refilling EP.

Mae June Cohen

Level 5 - Kolossos

HP - 240/240

EP - 208/560

15   Sanguin: This humor has a direct correlation to constitution and HP.

17   Coleric: This humor has a direct correlation to speed and agility.

15   Flegmat: This humor has a direct correlation to intellect and luck.

47   Melanc: This humor has a direct correlation to strength and EP.

Mighty Leap (Empeiros)

Squatting down for more than three seconds activates this skill. The force and angle of the leap can be decided before take off. This skill will scale with the Coleric and Melanc Humors and Acrobatics.

Raging Bull (Empeiros)

Sprinting for more than three seconds activates this skill. Upon activation, this skill provides a damage bonus based on momentum at the time of collision with another object. This skill will scale with the Coleric and Melanc Humors and Athletics. Damage multiplied by two for reaching an advanced skill rank.

Ballistos (Empeiros)

You can imbue up to ten Energy Points (EP) to any thrown objects. The force of the object's impact is multiplied by 20% for each EP imbued.

Thunderous Clap (Metrios)

You can slam your hands together with great force. This force is multiplied by each Energy Point (EP) you use to activate the skill. You can use up to ten EP in each use. Each point will add one second to activation time.

I refocused on the world around me and snapped out of my menu system. I smiled contentedly as I fell asleep. I didn't even think about the inevitable nightmare or what I'd remember about Felix that night. I just fell asleep happy.

I woke up to Medusa shaking me again. When she saw that I was awake, she gave me a moment to collect myself and sit up in the bed.

"What was it this time?" She asked.

"It was another one where I was seeing through Felix's eyes. Another thing that I didn't know had happened," I said.

"You didn't seem quite as troubled as the last time I woke you up," she said.

"That makes sense, I guess. Felix went to talk to the guy he had punched in the face when we were living in some apartments. Based on the state of the other guys' face, it wasn't too long after the incident. Standing at the man's open door, Felix apologized to the him and began to cry. It seemed so out of place and I think the man was confused more than anything. The man said that he forgave Felix, but his wife was still scared of him and said that she would like him to leave in the most polite way possible. The man nodded to his wife, but then stepped out onto the stairway landing with Felix and shut the door behind him. The man proceeded to have a very uncomfortable talk about how men are supposed to use their strength to help others and that their wives should see them as a safe space. Felix just stood there, silently taking in what Jimmy was saying before he said goodnight and stepped back into his apartment. I stood there as Felix. He was looking down the steps at the door to our apartment. The strangest thing was the rush of emotions. I think they were my husband's," I said.

Medusa just sat on the foot of the bed listening intently. After a few moments of silence she felt it was appropriate to coax a little more out of me.

"What did he feel?" She asked.

"Sadness, anger, regret, shame, guilt, and then rage. It wasn't directed at me though. He was feeling all these things toward himself. There was a lot mixed in and maybe some of the anger was at the situations that had broken him, but there was so much that I never knew was there. I honestly just thought he was dead inside. It was the last thing he said before he stepped back into our apartment that troubled me so much though," I said.

Medusa waited another moment to let me feel what I needed to feel. "What did he say?"

"He said that he loved me and then leaned his head and arm on the door quietly sobbing." I took a moment to just sit there and take in everything that I'd just seen and felt.

"I don't think that there is any excuse for how he treated you and your son, but it does sound like he was suffering in his own way for his actions," said Medusa.

"Good. He deserved to suffer," I said, but it felt wrong to speak those words. I hated the bitterness and how I still loved him during the worst of it. I hated how powerless he made me feel and how alone. I did want him to suffer, but I felt shame for saying it none-the-less.

"I'm sure he got what he deserved. I just worry that he's still hurting you, even now. Even though he's gone. He still has some strange power over you," said Medusa. I didn't like what she said, but she was right and it did make me angry. Not at her, but at him. I figured the best way to process some of this anger was to take it out on the remaining titans.

That's exactly what I did. It took me all day to finish them off. It was easy to ensure they were all dealt with as, after my last fight, the portals only brought me to barren wasteland. I hadn't counted, but I must've gained a couple thousand drachma from defeating the titans. Once I knew the trick to defeating each type, it was easy money and experience. I didn't really look at how many drachma I had, because I didn't have much of a use for it. It was nice to have it there if I needed it though.

My last exit through the portal had me smiling big. I was ready to start taking on the Mythics. I'd even gained another level toward the end of the day. I did my standard operating procedure and just point all five points into my Melanc humor for the added strength. I was already insanely strong. I could lift multiple tons based on the size of boulders I'd been able to throw. I was pleased with my stats as I looked over the updated information.

Mae June Cohen
Level 6 - Kolossos
HP - 250/250
EP - 73/620

15   Sanguin: This humor has a direct correlation to constitu‑ tion and HP.

17   Coleric: This humor has a direct correlation to speed and agility.

15   Flegmat: This humor has a direct correlation to intellect and luck.

52   Melanc: This humor has a direct correlation to strength and EP.

My energy points were lower than they'd been for a long time and I felt exhausted. It may have just been the mental exhaustion speaking, but I looked up at the ceiling and pleaded for no flashback of my life on earth.

"Please, just let me sleep. I don't want to think about Felix tonight." I stared up for a few more minutes and then slipped into a deep sleep. I woke up in the morning with no outside poking or prodding and I didn't recall any visions. I thanked the ceiling for the reprieve and then began moving toward Medusa's room. I was excited to give her the news as she had already gone to bed before I'd finished fighting the previous day.

The door was open and she wasn't in her room. She must wake up naturally early or something because she was routinely up before me. I barely woke up even with an alarm back on Earth and I rarely set one when I was at an advanced age. Sleep was a time where I didn't feel pain, so I got as much as possible. I started wandering and eventually found her sipping tea and reading a book in one of the gardens.

I sat on a bench across from her and took in a deep breath. I wasn't sure how this conversation would go. I really wanted her to stay out of danger for at least this first fight. I knew it might be difficult as I was planning on going after the Mythics she disliked the most first. I opened my mouth to speak, but she spoke before I could start.

"Hades thinks I should stay here while you fight the Mythics," said Medusa. She looked down as if she was ashamed to be suggesting the idea.

"What do you think?" I asked. I didn't want my opinion to influence hers.

"I think that I have full confidence in you being able to defeat them and I think I might get in the way. I mean, what if they get a hold of me and use me as a weapon against you. That would tear me apart. All that to say, I don't think it's a bad idea, but I also don't want you to feel like I'm abandoning you," she said.

"I was actually going to suggest that you stay here, if Hades is okay with that idea anyway. You seem like you are happy here," I said. I smiled and added, "Also, I don't think you'd ever abandon me. You're too good of a person to do something like that."

Hades walked into the garden where we sat. I wasn't sure how much he'd heard, but based on how he joined the discussion, he seemed to know what we were talking about.

"Medusa is welcome to stay here for as long as she'd like," said Hades.

"Thank you, Hades. We were planning on asking you that very thing. I've cleared out all of the titans. I think it is time to start relocating the Mythics," I said, standing up to my full height which now was slightly taller than Hades himself.

"You're taller again!" Said Medusa putting her book down the rest of the way and standing up as well. She seemed so much smaller than what she was when I first met her.

"Yes, you've grown in power and stature. I feel like you'll still need a bit of a boost to have the edge. To that end, I have one more gift for you. It's an enchanted ring that is usually utilized by builders and miners and I think you'll quickly see why you should have one," said Hades, as he pulled out small ring that was a dull, metallic red.

I grabbed the ring and equipped it onto another finger. It was definitely magic in nature as it resized itself and slipped on similar to the Tartarus portal ring. I didn't feel any different though. I waited for something to happen. Hades must've picked up on my confusion.

"You probably won't notice the difference unless you're lifting something," Hades said, pointing to a limestone bench that sat across from us in the garden.

I went over and picked up the bench. I wasn't surprised that I could lift it, but I was surprised at how light it felt. It must've weighed five hundred pounds, but it felt like five. We could see the Mistion Sea from this garden and I threw the bench as far as I could out into the distance. I lost sight of the bench before it landed, then I realized what I'd done in my excited state.

"I don't know why I threw it. I'm so sorry about your bench. I'll buy you a new one," I said, trying to make things right.

"Don't worry about it. That particular bench was carved by an artisan who is in the underworld currently," said Hades, still looking out at the water where I threw his bench.

"Oh, so he can just make you another one," said Medusa, trying to ease the tension as well.

"No. I meant that the artisan is dead and it doesn't work like that. I don't bring people back from that place," he said. He looked like even he was creeped out by the underworld.

"Well, I'm sorry about the bench, but I do appreciate the ring. There's no way I should've been able to do that. Even as strong as I am," I said, trying to move on.

"The enchantment on that ring is rare, but I was able to procure one off of a man who owned a construction business when he was alive. He would let his trusted employees utilize it during the building phase. It allowed regular people to move materials that they normally couldn't have dream of lifting. Whatever the wearer wills to pick up will only weigh about one percent of its original weight until the object is out of the ring wearer's possession. You can see how that would benefit a builder working with granite blocks, but there shouldn't be a limit to what the ring can assist with lifting. I thought that we may want to test my theory," said Hades, pointing to the western side of his island.

I wasn't sure what it meant, but he had his weird smile on his face, so I figured it would be something good.

Chapter 23

THE AGGRESSOR

We walked to the western part of the island following Hades's lead. The ring was called 'Ring of the Mermex' and did exactly what Hades had explained it did. I'd already felt the effects of wearing it from the bench experiment and it seemed like a great compliment to my enormous strength. As we crested the final hill, I could see exactly where Hades was taking us. Two massive marble statues stood in the distance. Neither of the statues were of Hades.

"These were gifts from my brothers. The statues are the quarter-sized models used when they were building their full sized counterparts. They sent these to me as a joke after they were through with them. They knew that I would have to find a special place for these if I didn't want to offend them. I built this place to house them as far from my palace and clients as possible. It would be a shame if someone destroyed them," said Hades. The sarcasm was dripping off the last thing he said. He clearly wanted me to destroy them as a test of my new item.

I lifted the marble statue of Zeus first. It was easily over three times my height and carved from a beautiful piece of marble. It felt like it weighed a few hundred pounds, which was no problem for me. I held it by the base and tossed it like I was in one of those Scottish competitions where they throw the log. The statue flipped end over end and landed with a loud crash against the rocky ground. It broke into multiple large chunks.

"Oh no. What a terrible thing that has happened to my prized statue," said Hades in a deadpan voice. He poked his head toward the other statue as if prodding me to continue.

I picked up a good-size piece of the Zeus statue and hurled it with both arms at the statue of Poseidon. I had put all ten EP into the throw after activating my Ballistos ability and the results were spectacular. I was able to throw the large chunk of granite with incredible speed because of its newfound lightness, but it hit with the same force as the piece at its regular weight. It gave me an idea for how to get Poseidon's attention. Hades was on board with my plan after I shared it with both of them. I was aboard a non-Hades marked vessel headed to Erimos within about an hour. We both thought we should keep his involvement a secret.

Leaving Medusa had been more difficult than I had thought, but she did seem genuinely happy there and Hades promised to keep her safe. We hugged and she wished me luck as I boarded the unknown ship. It wasn't long before I saw the statue of Poseidon that stood out over Erimos. This would be my first target. It was a massive statue and based on what Hades told me, it was just slightly bigger than the statue of Hades. It wouldn't be taller for long.

The boat docked off to the south of the main docks. This area seemed to be for local fishermen and possibly merchants. It was less flashy than the other docks we had passed on the way, but I could definitely disembark with fewer people seeing me. It was still my understanding that the element of surprise would be a great ally. At least for the first few attacks. I was sure that it wouldn't take long for changes to start happening once the Mythics were gone.

It was late afternoon by the time I got to the perfect place for my sneak attack. I was at a rocky outcropping with some large boulders that would be perfect for my needs. The statue was showing me a side profile from where I was standing, but here I was positioned to where any missed attacks would fall into the sea and not hurt anyone. I had my target and as far as I knew no one could see me.

I took a deep breath and threw my first attempt. I had activated Ballistos as I had plenty of EP to work with if I needed to take multiple shots. My projectile flew fast, but it didn't make contact with the statue. As I had hoped, the miss landed harmlessly in the sea and no one was the wiser. Ocean sounds tend to cover a lot of sneaky activities. On my third attempt the massive boulder, which weighed a small fraction of its total to me, struck the statue just above the left kneecap. It weighed a lot to the marble statue and the results were exciting to see. The knee buckled and the right leg snapped into multiple pieces which tumbled into the water. The weight of the top of the statue was too much for the remaining leg to support and the whole statue toppled away from the city of Erimos. It sank into the sea which I found to be fairly ironic since that was Poseidon's domain.

I moved east into the nearby woods and circled around the city to be seen entering from the north. When I got to the northern gate, I could see that the whole city was in an uproar. Two guards stopped me at the the gate.

"You may want to turn back. The statue of Poseidon has been destroyed, but the aggressor hasn't been caught yet. There may be danger in the city," said one of the guards.

"She can obviously take care of herself," said the more senior looking guard as he elbowed the first guard. Then, he turned to me and said, "You're free to enter."

I walked into the city smiling and knowing that I was once step closer. My first stop was the storehouse of Athena. I was hoping to get her out of the equation as quickly as possible and use my relative anonymity to my advantage. The storehouse was relatively easy to find. I walked up to the front doors and spoke with the guard who was stationed there.

"Is Athena here?" I asked. The man looked at me like I'd just asked a stupid question.

"She's always at the academy during the day. You must be new here," he said, as he pointed in the direction I should head.

"Thank you," I said. I started walking to the academy. Depending on how many people were around, it may be slightly more difficult to trick Athena into walking into a portal. It didn't take long to find the house of learning.

It wasn't like any educational institution I'd ever been around. It was mostly just an open space with groups of people gathered around one person who was standing on an elevated platform and speaking. There were quite a few of these platforms around the large building. I walked by a few of the groups and heard different philosophical ideas being presented. It all sounded familiar to things I had read in my studies, but the gathered people were intently listening.

I could easily pick Athena out of the crowd as she was head and shoulders taller than the townsfolk. She was standing toward the back of one of the groups. I walked up and stood next to her. The speaker was talking a lot, but not saying much. Athena looked uninterested in the topic anyway.

"Wealth consists not in having great possessions, but in having few wants," I whispered loud enough for her to hear. She turned and sneered at me, but was looking well below my eyeline. She must've thought it was one of the city's residents speaking. As her eyes scanned up to find mine, she smiled. I was taller than her and definitely more muscular.

"That's an interesting statement. What made you say it?" She asked.

"With the statue being destroyed, I just didn't know if the storehouses were safe. I just thought that it might be a good reminder," I said. Her sneer returned briefly. It seemed that the safety of her treasures were of more importance than anything else at the moment. I could see the gears turning in her head as she appraised me head to toe.

"Adventurer, come with me. You're big and strong. How'd you like to make some drachma for some protection duty? I assume that's why you came to find me." Athena waited for my answer as I pretended to think it over. I was hoping that she'd just think that I was just some muscle trying to capitalize on the attack.

"Absolutely, I'll follow you there," I said.

She began to walk toward her storehouse to get me introduced to the other guards that were in and around the building. We wouldn't make it that far if I got my way. I just needed an opening. We cut through an alley where there were no prying eyes. It was the perfect place for me to make my move.

"Athena, what if I told you that I knew who destroyed Poseidon's statue?" I asked. She stopped and turned toward me.

"What did you say?" She asked.

"What if I told you that I knew who destroyed Poseidon's statue?" I repeated.

She apparently didn't like the smile on my face. As she spat out her follow-up question with vitriol. "Who did it?"

"Me," I said, still smiling. I opened the portal to Tartarus just behind her as she was facing me. The portal covered the whole alley, so her only options were through it or through me. She was so focused on me that she had no idea that it was behind her. The rage on her face was evident, but she wasn't stupid. I was obviously stronger than her.

"Poseidon will deal with you," she said. She turned to run down the alley away from me but stumbled as she tried to stop after realized the portal blocked her path. I gave her the push she needed to make it through the portal and it snapped closed behind her. The only evidence that anything had happened was the small, golden scroll she had been carrying. I put it in my bag and smiled at my success. I wished that Medusa could've been here to see this, but I knew that she was safer where she was.

I didn't figure on Poseidon being quite so easy to deal with, but I felt good knowing that he wouldn't have any Mythic backup. I stepped out of the alley and went back to the main road. It was crazy to think that none of the other humans knew that Athena was not going to be asking for their tributes anymore. The power structure was going to change and I couldn't wait to witness it.

I went back to Athena's storehouse and addressed the guard at the door.

"Just between the two of us, What would you do if I told you that Athena was gone and wouldn't be coming back?" I asked. It looked like a lot of thoughts passed through his mind quickly before he chose his response.

"How do I know that you're not a spy and Athena is just testing my loyalty?" He asked.

"That's a good point, but I have no loyalty to Athena. I actually just banished her to Tartarus to begin to free people from the tributes they have to pay to the Mythics. Athena was just the first," I said, showing him the golden scroll. The man was surprised at first, but then it was like a weight had lifted.

"If that is true, I'd probably give you a hug. I used to work at the academy, but an accident happened that damaged some learning materials and I was blamed for it. Athena said they were costly and that I'd have to serve her to replace the materials. What can I do against a Mythic? So, I started working for her directly. I say working, but my wages barely get me enough to feed myself," the man said.

"Tell any other guards to vacate the premises and then start spreading the word that Athena is gone, but don't say anything about me. You and the rest of the people who worked for her directly can take whatever you'd like out of the storehouse to make up for your time here. When people don't see her for a while, they'll know that the rumors are true. It's vital that no one suspects me though," I said. The man held onto every word like it was precious to him. Then, he nodded vigorously and ran off to do as I said. I never did get that hug.

My next task was finding Poseidon. I didn't want to hang around Athena's storehouse for too long anyway. I walked down the main road through town again and asked a beggar where Poseidon's storehouse was. I gave him a drachma for the information which was probably the easiest money he'd ever made. He pointed me in the right direction and I left him with an additional offer.

"If I give you another drachma, would you spread a rumor without telling anyone where you heard it?" I asked with a wink.

"Of course. You have my word," he said. I handed him the second coin.

"Athena is gone. No one will have to pay tributes to her any longer. That is what I'd like you to spread,"

I said gleefully. He didn't match my enthusiasm. I could tell that he was debating internally.

"That could be a very dangerous rumor," he said finally.

"Only if it wasn't true," I said. I produced two more drachma and handed them to him with a nod.

"By days end, all the poor will know and word will spread quickly from there." He was resolute in his response. I nodded again, smiled, and went on my way. He just made four days' wages in less than five minutes and I was happy that we were able to help each other.

I arrived at Poseidon's storehouse down by the up-scale docks after descending a long stone staircase that was built into the massive stone seawall that was a few stories tall. I could tell that something was fishy. It was quiet, too quiet. There was no guard at the door and the docks themselves were relatively cleared out. I really thought that there would be more ships or at least more people. Glancing around for a few minutes didn't make me feel any better about the situation. I then took a peak into the front entrance of the storehouse and it was also empty.

"Where is everyone?" I asked myself as I closed the storehouse door and turned back toward the sea.

"I sent the ships out to look for whoever destroyed my statue. Initial searches weren't able to locate any stone throwing equipment on land, so that was the next logical area to search. I have a better question. Why are you somewhere you're not supposed to be? Only my personal guard is allowed into my store-house," said the deep voice of Poseidon. He was about twenty-five feet from me, but had been moving closer. He wasn't walking though. There was a platform of water that he was standing on that moved him around.

"That's a neat trick with the water," I said, not knowing what else to say.

"I asked you a question," he said, more firm than before. Like I was a child caught with my hand in the cookie jar.

"I'm right where I'm supposed to be," I said in defiance.

Chapter 24

THE HERO

A ten-foot-wide beam of water shot out from behind Poseidon. It hit me squarely and sent me flying back into the stone sea wall. I hit at a weird angle and then fell to the ground. It didn't hurt, but it was a surprise. The water moved faster than I thought possible and with more force. I stood and immediately crashed against the sea wall with another water strike.

"Okay, I'm nice and clean now. Thank you," I said, before standing up again.

"You think you're pretty tough, huh?" He said with a smirk. "Water isn't my only weapon."

He threw his trident at me and it struck around my midsection. It did little more than push me back a pace which was disappointing to say the least in Poseidon's eyes. The look of anger mixed with confusion on his face was priceless. I tossed the weapon to the side and a prehensile spout of water grabbed it and returned it to Poseidon's outstretched hand.

"Okay, I have to admit that a rope of water that can hand you things is very neat," I said, genuinely impressed. This made him angry and he decided to try again with the trident.

The weapon hit me ineffectively, but before it could be retrieved, I grabbed it and threw it back at him. A spout of water intercepted the projectile and knocked it to the side. The water brought the trident back to him again.

We both needed some new tactics, but all this water manipulation had to be draining his Energy Points. That's really all I needed to do was to make him run out of energy and then toss him into a portal while he was knocked out. That seemed like a good plan to me anyway. I just had no idea how many EP he had or how much he was using.

I few more water jets bashed me into the wall, but were more annoying than harmful. I wasn't able to dodge them, but it didn't take any EP to let them hit me, so I just did that. Poseidon was getting noticeably more and more irritated, but that just made me smile. It was a vicious cycle.

In between water jets, I made my way over to one side of the tall stone wall where a large, metal anchor was leaning against the opposite building. I wasn't sure if it was decorative or being repaired, but I knew it would be heavy. I picked it up with ease, spun it around me once, and released it on a collision course with Poseidon. I was correct in assuming that a spout of water wouldn't be enough to stop the anchor's forward momentum. Poseidon had full confidence in his water defense.

The anchor struck the Mythic with a nasty thud and he flew back at least fifty feet into the sea. It wouldn't really hurt him, but it was fun at least to be on the offensive for a bit. My enjoyment didn't last long as the water under the docks began to recede a moment later. It continued to recede until I could see Poseidon standing out on ground with a wall of water behind him. I wasn't really scared, but I did have a visceral reaction to the incredible sight. I'd never seen a tsunami and now I was going to experience one first hand.

The wall of water crashed down around me and swept me off of my feet. I was swirling in a riptide in a way that I didn't really enjoy. I think it was the complete lack of control I felt. I didn't like not having my feet on solid ground.

The various whirlpools and quick moving water jerked me around for a few more minutes as it pushed me to the bottom of the sea. I finally settled there and the water calmed. I'm sure Poseidon thought I had drown, but him making the water pull me to the bottom just helped orient me. The sea floor beneath me felt solid and I surmised that the movement of the water cleared the sand off a large area of stone. I got into a squatting position and briefly pulled up my map to ensure I was facing toward Erimos. I hadn't activated Mighty Leap underwater before, but I was hoping that with my elevated stats I could make it to the surface.

I pushed off and flew through the water like a torpedo. A huge geyser of water erupted from the water's surface as I passed through it and back into the mid-afternoon sun. I had just enough oomph to make if back to the docks and Poseidon stood there staring at me annoyed, but maybe a little scared as well.

"How?" Was all the Mythic could say.

"Like this," I said, as I squatted down. He just watched not knowing what I'd do. He tried to ready himself as I jumped farther into the sky than I ever had before. Poseidon was standing at the edge of the main dock close to the shore. I reach the apex of my leap and was able to fix my body into a cannonball type pose. I slammed down moments later right next to the Mythic. The dock splintered into pieces and both of us struck the sand and rocks below. He stood first, grabbed me by my hair, and pulled my face up. I knew from experience what would come next.

Poseidon threw a punch squarely into may face and I flew backward. I was twirling in the air like a thrown doll, until I slammed into the seawall once again. This last strike threw me into a rage. Felix never hit me like that, but the look in Poseidon's eyes was familiar. All the times Felix lost it flashed back into my mind. I wasn't always his target, but I remembered that face. I got to my feet and yelled louder and longer than I ever had before. It wasn't aimed at Poseidon necessarily, it was a release of all the anger and hurt that I'd carried for decades.

Poseidon was running over to finish the job, but my fists had another option in mind. He stabbed with his trident, but I ducked under it and countered with the strongest uppercut I could manage. The punch caught the now tired Mythic in the jaw and sent him flying into the air. He landed about twenty feet away, sprawled onto his back. His trident slipped out of his hand as he flew away from me and it clattered onto the ground.

I heard a single cheer from up the seawall. I looked and a line of faces poking over the edge could be seen over the top of the wall. Apparently, our fight had drawn a crowd. I didn't know who cheered, but it made me smile. I picked up his trident and smacked him across the face with it like his head was a golf ball. He tumbled to the side following the momentum of the blow and a few more cheers rang out from above. I threw his trident with all my might to the east and it went soaring over the seawall and far from the sea. He wouldn't be retrieving it during this fight. I imagined that it would land somewhere in the mountains to the east of Erimos.

Poseidon got up and we exchanged punches back and forth, but I was just letting him use up his remaining EP. He had one more trick up his sleeve as he had positioned me closest to the sea with my back to it. A shark leapt from the water and attempted to chomp into my back. Since his teeth couldn't penetrate my skin he just kind of moved his jaw and then flopped to the ground. I looked at the shark like I was more disappointed than angry, but I knew it was Poseidon's fault and not the shark's.

I tossed the shark back into the sea to make sure he didn't get hurt because of Poseidon. Someone cheered for that too. Must've been another animal lover up there. Poseidon threw a couple more punches, but the shark trick must've cost him some of his few remaining Energy Points. He was teetering on the edge of consciousness.

"Who are you?" He asked. His words were soft and there was even more fear in his voice.

"I'm a friend of Medusa's," I said. The spent Mythic dropped to his knees after throwing one last punch that barely had enough force to push me back a half step. More cheering erupted from above as Poseidon's body slumped harmlessly to the ground. People started running down the stone steps and cheers were breaking out even louder than before.

I smiled and stared at the fallen Mythic. He was only out cold and would eventually be able to get up once he had recovered some EP, I figured that I had a little time to enjoy my victory. Dozens of people gathered around behind me as they got to the bottom of the seawall steps. More were coming behind them and soon there were at least fifty with even more coming. I turned to make sure that they knew that I wasn't a threat to them, but they already knew that Poseidon had been the greater threat.

The people grew dead silent and I knew that they were waiting for me to say something.

"People of Erimos, Poseidon and Athena have been defeated. No more tributes will be paid to the Mythics of this town," I shouted out to the crowd.

Some clapped, but some still looked at me with doubt. I opened a portal, picked up Poseidon, tossed him into Tartarus, and closed the portal in quick succession. This took away any doubts that remained. The people exploded into a cacophony of cheers and clapping. Multiple people were crying. These must've been the ones that had the most to gain from this new development.

"Three cheers for the hero of Erimos!" Shouted one of the townsfolk. The trio of loud cheers filled the whole area. I wished that Medusa could have seen this. I know that she would've been one of the crying ones. Athena and Poseidon had hurt her in many ways, but she had been avenged.

"Divide up all of the riches in the storehouse however you like. This town belongs to you now," I said. The cheers rose up again and people began to pull treasures from the storehouse. "Spread the word that no more tributes are to be paid to Poseidon and Athena, but don't tell anyone who defeated the Mythics. I still have work to do and surprise is my ally."

A teenage boy spoke up in response to what I'd said. "We don't know what you are called anyway. You never gave us your name."

"You're right. I didn't give you my name, but the Hero of Erimos has a nice ring to it," I said to the spirited teen.

"The Hero of Erimos!" Shouted another townsperson who heard what I said. The people began cheering again even louder this time and then began chanting the moniker in unison. I raised my fist up in victory as they cheered. I never felt power like this with Felix even after he died. I liked it and I wanted more.

AFTERWORD

The End

The story will continue in book two of the Mae Trilogy. If you enjoyed this book, please leave a review. It would mean the world to me and it really helps others decide to give it a chance.

If you want to learn a little more about Mae, you can read the series that started it all.

The full series called Afterlife Quest: Theodore Saga is available now.

The Denial of Theodore
The Stain of Guilt
Raging on the Sea
Depression in the Ground
The Acceptance of Theodore

www.ingramcontent.com/pod-product-compliance
Lightning Source LLC
Chambersburg PA
CBHW050018120726
47903CB00006B/1813